The Restless

by Geoffrey Sleight

I have never yet heard of a murderer who was not afraid of a ghost.
John Philpot Curran

CHAPTER 1

GARETH Richards did not want to go on summer holiday to Falcombe Sands seaside resort. It held a terrible secret memory for him, and he never wanted to visit the place again.

His wife Melanie had a completely different view of the resort on Britain's south coast. She'd been there on holiday with her parents and younger sister, Marilyn, when she was ten-years-old, and the setting of sun, sea and building sand castles on the beach had remained fondly in her memory.

Gareth suggested several other locations for their summer holiday, so he could avoid spending time there. But Melanie insisted it would be ideal for their eight-year-old twin daughters, Amelia and Sophie, where they'd be able to enjoy a great time just like she did as a child.

Her husband eventually realised he'd have to give way in the matter, and reluctantly agreed to his wife's choice. In the meantime he would need to keep hiding his dread of the resort, which even now was starting to grip him as he recalled memory of the horrific crime he'd committed there ten years earlier.

"Why are you so against going there?" Melanie asked.

"Am I?" Gareth batted away the suggestion he had something against the place. "Just thought other resorts would be better. But if you want to go, it's okay by me," he added grudgingly.

Melanie was serving up dinner in the kitchen of their white rendered, semi-detached three-bedroom house at

Camden in north London. Gareth was gathering cutlery from a drawer to take into the dining room.

"Well don't trip over yourself with enthusiasm," she remarked, dishing spaghetti bolognese with vegetarian mince for herself and the girls on to plates, and meat for her husband.

"How long is it before we go?" Sophie and Amelia asked eagerly, sitting in the dining room as their parents placed the meals on the table.

The youngsters inherited their mother's engaging amber eyes and auburn hair. Gareth's genes had bestowed them with his straight edged nose.

"In a week's time, yippee!" Melanie waved both arms in the air with excitement matching the glee in the girls' eyes. A reluctant smile raised Gareth's brown beard. He didn't want to dampen their spirits.

For his wife and daughters, time seemed to slow down in their anticipation of the holiday in a self-catering chalet on the Dorset coast. For Gareth it speeded up, as the approaching break intensified his memory of the gruesome incident that had taken place there ten years ago, and which until now had been fading from his mind. It was a guilty secret he could never share with Melanie or anyone else.

At work, as senior accountant at a global security services company, his mind was now continually distracted by the memory of the past event. He wished he could find an excuse not to go on holiday with his family this time, but he couldn't let down his wife and children like that, he knew

Finally, the day for the three-hour drive to Falcombe Sands arrived.

The journey, in a red hatchback, was accompanied by frequent choruses from the girls at the back of "are we nearly there yet?"

"For God's sake shut up," their father shouted from the driving seat, his nerves growing on edge as they neared the resort. The youngsters were stunned, as if a bucket of cold water had suddenly been thrown over their bonfire of joy.

"Gareth! They're just excited," his wife beside snapped.

He shook his head knowing he should have contained his anxiety.

"Sorry girls," he said.

"Daddy didn't mean to upset you," Melanie turned her head to see their sad faces, "but he needs to concentrate. So keep quiet for a little longer." She smiled, and they looked happier.

After a few more miles they turned off the main road and continued a short distance along a tree lined lane, with another turning that led to their resort accommodation. Gareth pulled up on the tarmac track in front of their chalet, all of them glancing for a moment at its wood exterior, with triangular pitched eaves extending forward over the front door and first floor balcony.

Several more similar chalets with driveways were spaced in a line about a forty yards apart, all facing the entrance track to the site. The field beyond the properties overlooked a strip of the sea visible towards the horizon.

3

After studying the surrounds of their new base for the week, Gareth completed the journey turning into their driveway.

"Look mummy!" Amelia cried as they began taking luggage from the boot. "We could have picnics there," she pointed to a bench table on the lawn in front of the chalet.

"Yes, and we could have them on the beach too," her mother enthused.

"I'd like that," Sophie piped in, clutching a small green case containing her favorite cuddly toy rabbit, and few other soft toys she'd insisted taking on holiday.

The front door opened on to the living/dining room and compact kitchen. Melanie and Gareth put down their suitcases and glimpsed the setting with wood paneling all around.

It contained a dining table with four chairs, and the spread of a yellow U-shaped fabric sofa facing the television attached to the wall. Beneath stood a three-drawer pine unit. At the far end of the room a staircase led to the first floor.

"Are the bedrooms up there?" called Sophie, pointing at the stairs.

"Can I have the biggest one?" Amelia claimed her stake before Sophie had a chance. The sisters began to squabble.

"You are both sharing a bedroom," Melanie brought the argument to a conclusion. For a second both girls appeared disappointed, then accepted their mother's ruling.

"If you're good, we'll go to the beach and you can have ice creams after we finish unpacking a few things. Now the girls' excitement was fully restored.

Upstairs another argument began brewing between the youngsters, this time about who would have the top or bottom bunk bed.

"You can swap round each night," Melanie ruled again, pointing out that their bedroom had a view across the field to the sea beyond, which pleased them.

After a late lunch of omelettes, Melanie and Gareth began packing items for the beach, while the girls went up to their bedroom to change into colourful tops and shorts for the outing.

"I think I'll give it a miss today," he announced suddenly. It took her by complete surprise as she placed a bottle of sunscreen in the beach bag.

"What?"

"It was a long drive, and I think I'll just take a rest for now," he answered.

"But the girls will be so disappointed. You know how much they like playing games with you."

"I know, and I don't like to disappoint them. But I don't feel up to it right now. I'll go tomorrow. The weather forecast's good for a while, there'll be plenty of time." Gareth's opting out guilt was manifest, avoiding eye contact with his wife.

"It isn't anything to do with feeling tired, is it?" Melanie probed. "There's something about coming to Falcombe Sands that's making you feel uneasy, isn't there? You seemed very reluctant to come on holiday here."

"Well I thought there were better resorts we could go to," Gareth defended the reason for his reluctance. His wife continued to stare disapproval. What was he hiding?

5

"Right, well come on girls, let's go to the beach," she turned, seeing them now standing by the front door in their beachwear. The youngsters stared at their parents with puzzled expressions, detecting they didn't appear happy.

"Daddy's feeling tired, he's going to rest for now, but he's promised to come to the beach tomorrow," Melanie explained. Gareth's guilt at letting them down deepened.

"You have fun now. I'll build sand castles and play games with you tomorrow," he pledged. They appeared puzzled, sensing something was troubling their father.

Outside the chalet Melanie had started placing the beach bag in the car boot, when a young woman in white shorts and patterned sea shells top approached on the drive.

"Hello," she began. "I'm Olivia, staying in the chalet next to you with my partner Steve," she pointed to the property. Melanie introduced herself and the girls.

"If you're going to the beach, there's a short cut over there," Olivia indicated a field facing the chalet, with a footpath a short distance away leading to an opening between a row of trees. "It only takes about ten minutes, and saves you having to hunt for a parking space near the beach." Melanie thanked her for the steer.

"Come on girls, the walk will do us good," she said, retrieving the bag from the car boot.

"If you run short of anything, just let us know," Olivia called, as they set off. Melanie returned another thanks.

****

GARETH made a coffee and rested the mug on the breakfast counter dividing the kitchen from the living/dining area. He was feeling a little tired, but not so much that he couldn't have spent time with his family on the beach.

Primarily the cause was fear. Fear that going near the seafront would invoke yet more vividly the memory of that dreadful event a decade ago.

It had been a long drive, and he decided to have a short rest. Picking up the mug, he began approaching the living room sofa. A sound from upstairs froze his steps. A thud as if something had fallen on the floor. For a few moments he remained still, listening for any further sound. Silence resumed.

Something placed on the edge of a dresser or table might have fallen off. It could happen sometimes even with the slightest vibration in a place, reasoned Gareth. There was a soap dish attached by suction pads on the side of the shower at home. Occasionally the suction lost grip and clattered on the base. Gareth's reasoning for the noise revealed the fear he was attempting to suppress, but he felt duty bound to investigate.

His heart began rapidly pumping. Was that terrible thing he'd done at Falcombe Sands all those years ago coming to haunt him?

"Who's there?" he called, cautiously climbing the stairway. Reaching the top, he stopped to listen again, his heart pumping even more furiously, set almost to burst from his chest.

The continuing silence was broken only by the cry of a seagull coming through the open doorway of the children's bedroom. Still wary of an intruder's presence, he slowly crept along the landing to their room and looked inside. The window was open, swinging back and forth in gusts of wind. A few cuddly toys were scattered on the lower bunk bed, and the wardrobe door was ajar. He crossed the room to close the window.

Growing confident there was no-one else in the property, Gareth carried on carefully checking the other rooms, his normal heart beat beginning to return. The last bedroom he searched was the one he shared with his wife. After assuring himself it was empty too, he opened the French doors on to the balcony, stepping out. From here he could see the ocean above the line of treetops. The uplifting view of cliffs stretching away on each side of the seascape made him feel robbed of enjoying the holiday with his family. The visit tainted by memory of the past.

There was no detectable sign of a fallen object that could have caused the thud sound, other than perhaps the open window in the children's bedroom swinging in the wind and hitting the frame. That was a more reassuring explanation to Gareth, though his nerves remained edge.

****

THE girls were highly excited as they entered the chalet on returning from the beach.

"We had ice creams," chirped Sophie, leaping on to the sofa beside her father, who'd spent much of his time lost in a trance, his mind re-enacting that past event at the resort.

"Did you?" he struggled to summon an enthusiastic reply.

"Yes, and there's the funfair near the beach, where we went on some rides," Amelia added eagerly, joining Gareth on his other side.

Melanie closed the door and placed the beach bag on the floor.

"I could murder an orange juice," she called to Gareth. "Our neighbour showed us a good short cut to the beach from here, but it's a steep climb back up the path."

Gareth stretched his arms across the girls' shoulders, and gave them a hug.

"Now I'd better get the drink for your mum," he said, releasing the youngsters from his grasp.

"Can we have one too?" they chorused.

"Come on then," he stood up and they followed him across to the kitchen.

"We'll have our drinks, then we can freshen up with showers," Melanie instructed the girls, taking a brief rest on the sofa. When they'd finished the drinks, she ordered them upstairs to get ready, remaining for a moment to speak to Gareth, joining him at the breakfast counter where he was drinking his orange.

"The children asked me a few times why you're looking so unhappy," she said.

"Do they think I'm unhappy?" he appeared surprised.

"Well you don't exactly seem overjoyed to be here," she replied, placing her empty glass on the counter. "You've been on a downer ever since I suggested coming here," she paused. "Have you got something against this resort?"

"No," Gareth answered. His reply sounded a little more forceful than a normal reply would warrant, thought Melanie, as if he was hiding something.

"I just felt from the photos you showed me before we came that there were better resorts we could go to," he defended himself, lowering his eyes. The reaction confirmed to her he was not being totally honest.

"Well I like it here," she said. "The seafront's changed a bit since I was as a child, some new shops and buildings, but it's still a good place with a sandy beach and safe swimming in the sea. Our children seem to love it too."

"Okay, well that's good," Gareth worked at raising a smile again. "If you're all happy, I'll go along with that."

Melanie turned, preparing to go upstairs, but stopped turning back. "Look, I don't know what it is that's bugging you, but please, for the children's sake, at least pretend you're having a good time. They are worried that you're unhappy, and I don't want it to spoil their holiday."

"I promise," he agreed. Melanie shook her head, making her way to the stairs.

CHAPTER 2

THE BEACH was rapidly filling with holidaymakers in colourful swimwear, shorts and tops, as Sophie and Amelia, skipping occasionally, led their parents across the golden bay sands, eager to make castles, play ball games and swim in the sea.

Heat from the summer sun was raising the temperature to minimal clothing, even before it had reached a quarter way to zenith in the cloudless blue sky.

"Come back children, we're going to pitch here on the beach," Melanie called to the girls as they enthusiastically steamed on ahead. She placed a bag on the sand beside Gareth's, claiming a family space before the continuing beach arrivals left little room to settle on the shore.

Behind the setting, Falcombe town on the south Devon coast rose upwards from the bay, houses, bungalows and apartment buildings over looking the seafront. Along the promenade a variety of restaurants and fast food outlets, beach equipment stores, ice cream kiosks and cafes were making the most of the visiting trade.

The expansive sands reached the curved borders of rock cliffs at each end. The blue of the sky reflected on the softly rippling waves fading into the misty horizon. Children and adults filled the shoreline, swimming, paddling and bobbing in inflatable dinghies, all to the mixed cries of enjoyment spreading everywhere.

Melanie and Gareth laid out beach mats and removed buckets and spades, a ball and starfish sand moulds for the children. They'd all arrived in swimwear, and Melanie insisted on everyone coating themselves with copious amounts of sunscreen.

Gareth glanced across to the cliff border on the left side of the shore, which hid the inlet of a marina just beyond. The place where it began. Even in the growing heat, a chill came over him.

"Are you with us?" Melanie snapped, noting his trance like gaze in the direction.

"Yes, just looking round," he excused his distraction. "Seems a decent enough place."

"You're obviously overwhelmed with joy about being here," she delivered sarcastically.

"Daddy, will you play with us?" The girls had started a game of catch with their ball.

Gareth did their bidding, though his mind not entirely fixed on playing, as he continued occasionally to glance in the direction of the hidden marina.

****

AFTER games, sand castle building and a swim in the sea, Melanie suggested it was time for ice creams. Gareth made his way to the nearest ice cream kiosk on the promenade to buy them.

As he waited in the queue to be served, he glanced in the direction of the marina again, now able to see the tops of masts from the higher vantage point above the beach.

The sight made him turn away, attempting to stem the surge of dread that struck. Of all the resorts in the country,

Falcombe Sands had to be the most favourite childhood memory that his wife wanted to revisit with their own children. Just his luck he grumbled to himself.

Soon, with ice cream cornets purchased, Gareth began making his way back to the beach, carrying them in a cardboard holder. Carefully descending the stone steps from the promenade on to the sand, he weaved between the crowds playing ball games, disc throwing, sand shaping and youngsters running around.

Nearing his family settled on the mats, his eyes caught sight of a figure several beach games away who was waving and attempting to attract his attention.

Gareth's jaw widened, he stared in disbelief, the strength in his legs began draining and his hands lost grip of the ice cream carrier, sending the contents twirling head first into the sand.

"Are you okay?" a young man rushed over to him, noticing him wobbling and on the verge of collapse. Others nearby stopped playing games and came crowding round him to see if they could help.

"No, I'm fine," said Gareth, patently pale and not looking fine. "I'll be alright," he began regaining leg strength.

Melanie and the children had seen him tottering. She told the girls to follow, not wishing to leave them alone, and they crossed the short distance to him.

"It's okay, I'm his wife," she announced, making her way through the circle of onlookers surrounding Gareth, and placing her arm around his shoulders. The youngsters' faces were drawn in concern.

At first Melanie thought he'd tripped on something when she first saw him nearing. But seeing the gathered crowd, and now his drained face, she became concerned he might be suffering from something serious.

"Do you want me to find a doctor, call the emergency service?" Melanie had never seen him looking so rundown.

"No," Gareth protested, "I'll be okay. Just need to rest for a minute."

He saw the worry in the girl's faces, and reached out with his hand to briefly stroke each head. "Don't worry, your dad will be fine," he assured them.

"Come and sit down," Melanie guided him through the dissolving crowd back to their beach pitch.

"Are you alright daddy?" the girls enquired, as their mother settled Gareth on the beach mat.

"Yes, don't worry," he re-assured.

"Just let daddy rest for a while," said Melanie. "He'll be okay in a minute.

"Do you want to go back to the chalet," she asked him.

"No, we'll stay. Don't want to spoil the girls' fun."

"If you're feeling a little better then, I'll go and get some ice creams for us, but only if that's okay with you."

"Yes," he nodded. "I don't want to spoil our day on the beach," a weak smile struggled to rise in his beard.

Something about Falcombe Sands was definitely troubling him, Melanie felt sure. But now was not the time to probe.

****

WHEN they'd all showered back at the chalet, Gareth drove them to a fast food restaurant on the seafront, a favourite treat promised to the youngsters.

Melanie noticed how her husband continued to be preoccupied in thought, only half joining in with conversation.

"Sorry, what did you say?" he frequently repeated. This time after being asked by Sophie and Amelia if he was feeling any better, and was he enjoying his beefburger and chips, which he'd been eating in a slow, unwanted way.

"I think daddy is still feeling tired," Melanie told them, trying to stop them continuing to worry about his distant manner.

Gareth could never say why his mind was distracted. That figure he'd seen on the beach could not possibly have existed. He thought the whole business had ended long ago. How could he possibly ever tell his wife what had happened? It would be too shocking for her.

Back at the chalet, when the children had settled to bed, Melanie planned to diplomatically approach the subject, as she sat down beside him on the sofa preparing to watch television with him.

"There's something troubling you, and I wish you'd tell me what it is?" she began. "Perhaps I can help."

Gareth didn't immediately reply. He reached out for the glass of beer on the small table beside him, and took a drink.

"Nothing in particular," he lied. "I'm just a bit rundown. Had a lot of pressure at work lately, and it takes a while to shake it off and relax. That's all."

Melanie knew it wasn't really the whole truth. Yes, he did have a pressured job, but this was something different. He usually carried work pressure in his stride.

"Are you sure it's just work and not something else?" she asked. "You can tell me. You know I'll always support you."

"For Christ's sake, leave it alone! I don't want to discuss anything," he exploded. "I had a bit of a turn on the beach. Don't make a mountain out of it." His fury told Melanie to pursue it no further for now. Another time.

****

GARETH no longer wished to spend any more time at the holiday resort, and considered telling his wife and daughters that since he wasn't feeling very well, he would catch a train back home and continue to let them enjoy their break.

But troubled as he was by seeing that figure on the beach, he couldn't bring himself to desert them. Though if the person appeared again, he would have to leave immediately.

"You seem a lot better," Melanie told Gareth as they sat on the beach a few days later, the children nearby digging holes and making sand castles.

"Yes, I feel better," he replied, settling on his back to relax in the continuing sunshine.

The family had also visited the local funfair, enjoyed more ices and meal treats, and observed anemones, hermit crabs and limpets in some of the rock pools at the base of the cliffs on each side of the beach.

Gareth began to conclude the unwelcome person he'd seen on the beach had been a figment of his imagination That harrowing memory resurfacing as a phantom without substance.

But when Melanie suggested they take a stroll around the nearby marina to look at the yachts and motorboats, Gareth excused himself by saying he felt a little tired again, and would return to the chalet for a short rest. The marina was definitely a place he never wanted to visit again.

CHAPTER 3

ON the day they returned home, Melanie was happy the holiday had turned out well. Gareth was glad the figure he'd seen on the beach hadn't reappeared, and the girls certainly enjoyed a great fun time. Life was looking up.

Midweek, a fortnight after their return, the new term began for the children, and seeing them safely into the school premises, Melanie made the ten minute drive back home in her blue saloon car.

Occasionally she went into the office several underground train stops away. It was faster using the train than becoming snarled up in central London traffic jams. But most of the time she worked at home, processing sales data for an international insurance group, remotely connecting online.

Apart from video conferencing, she could usually dress down in comfortable clothes, presently in a white top and green shorts, helping her to remain cool in the stifling summer humidity shrouding the capital.

Leaving the hissing coffee machine dispensing a latte into the cup, she entered the living room to pick up a work folder she'd left on the cream leather sofa. She jumped back in shock seeing a man sitting beside it.

"Sorry if I've frightened you," he said in a soft voice. Melanie stood rigid, taking in his dark brown swept back hair, firm jawline and clean shaven face. His eyes gleamed friendliness.

"Who are you? How did you get in?" Melanie demanded, finding her fear reverting to anger at the intrusion.

"I just found a way in," he replied.

"Well you can just find a way out," she stormed, approaching him.

"It's Daniel. Don't you remember me? Daniel Merriman."

Melanie studied his face again. Nothing stirred a memory of him.

"How do you know my name?" she demanded.

"Our last meeting was about ten years or so ago. Remember? At a party I was throwing in my flat."

Melanie continued to stare, delving further back in memory. Neither the face, or his black jeans and blue open neck shirt stirred any recall of the stranger.

"Gareth and me were great friends, working at the same place. Sometimes we'd all go nightclubbing and partygoing together. Remember? Before you both got married," he attempted to jog her memory.

Daniel seemed disappointed she had no recollection of that past, and he was finding it difficult to explain the way in which his situation had changed since they last met. He didn't want to traumatize her. And with her having no recollection of him, there seemed little reason to do so.

"Look, I've no idea who you are, or how you got in here, but if you don't leave now I'll call the police," Melanie warned, hoping it would encourage the man to go.

He gazed round the room, the white coving and soft blue walls, window shutters, a potted peace lily on a glass fronted cabinet. He turned his head to look at Melanie again. "I can't think Gareth would be much good at looking after plants," he grinned.

"Will you please leave," Melanie insisted firmly, now seriously in a mind to call the police.

"You're both lucky to have such wonderful daughters. You've been blessed with them since I knew you and Gareth those years back. And they certainly had a good holiday at Falcombe Sands," the visitor continued.

Melanie was puzzled. She had no idea how this total stranger knew Gareth, but her feelings were starting to mix with anger and fear at the intrusion. How did he know they had daughters? Why was he mentioning them? Could their safety be at risk? How did he know where they'd been on holiday?

Fearing danger, Melanie was now going to put her plan of calling the police into action. Her phone was in the kitchen. She left to get it, starting to call as she re-entered the room. But the stranger had gone. She stopped dialling.

Checking he hadn't sneaked into another room, Melanie searched round the house. She was certain the front door, windows and garden door from the kitchen had been locked while she'd been out. He was no longer present.

Her mind grappled with the mystery. How did he get in? Maybe there was a flaw in their security. His mention of the children unsettled her greatly. Was he a predator? Were they safe? She rang her husband to report what had happened.

"He's in a meeting right now. I'll get him to call you back when it's finished," a woman in his department told her.

"It's important. Can you interrupt the meeting?" Melanie pressed.

"I'll see," the woman replied.

Five minutes later Gareth called. Melanie explained there'd been an intruder.

"Are you sure the doors and windows were locked?"

"Of course," she replied.

"I'm involved in a very important meeting at the moment. Can we talk about it later. Just be sure to keep all the windows and doors locked," he advised. "I'll try to get away early."

Keeping everything closed did not make for comfortable conditions in the muggy summer heat, and the desk fan in the small upstairs room converted into an office hardly provided the most effective cooling. But security was foremost after the intrusion.

****

BEFORE Gareth rejoined the meeting after speaking to his wife, he remained in the corridor outside puzzling over what she'd told him.

"He says you're an old friend. That he knew you and me years ago," he recalled Melanie's description of the intruder. Gareth had wanted her to explain more, but the meeting door opened and an assistant popped his head round, silently mouthing for him to return quickly. An unsettled feeling began to creep over him.

Gareth didn't get home until evening. Discussions about a possible merger with another company led to a series of meetings during the day, keeping managers and senior staff at work after normal closing time.

"Daddy," the children greeted him as he entered the house. "Will you come and read us a bedtime story in a minute?" they pleaded. Computer games had their place, but it had become a tradition for Gareth to read them a story before they settled for the night.

"I've had a very busy day," he told them, "so it will have to be a very short story," he said.

"Now leave daddy alone for a moment," Melanie entered the hallway, where Gareth was resting his hands on the girls' shoulders, telling them to go upstairs and get ready for bed.

"I've ordered a pizza takeaway like you messaged. Should be here soon," Melanie told him as they entered the kitchen. She set the coffee machine into hissing life.

"Actually, I think I'll have something a little stronger than coffee," he said, wanting to relax his nerves after the frenetic day, and especially from the news Melanie had delivered in her call that morning.

She followed him into the living room, where he took a bottle of whisky and a glass from the drinks cabinet, pouring himself a generous amount of the gold liquid. Then he flopped on to the sofa.

"I'm bloody exhausted," he uttered, taking a large swig of the alcohol.

"And I'm bloody worried about that strange man who I found in the house," Melanie returned firmly, standing beside the sofa.

"Yes, I haven't forgotten," he said. Her brief description of the event had been pushed aside while he needed to concentrate on work. He'd felt reassured she was safe in the meantime with the windows and doors locked. Melanie had also phoned a friend and asked her to collect the children from school, so that she didn't need to leave the house unoccupied again for the time being.

Gareth's thoughts had not been entirely focused on the meetings. They kept drifting back to the past. Paramount in them was the figure that had appeared on the beach during their holiday at Falcombe Sands. Surely that wasn't coming back to plague him?

"The man said he knew us from years ago," Melanie appeared mystified, wondering if her husband could supply an answer.

"I know you said," Gareth took another drink, placing the glass on the small table beside the sofa.

He felt a reluctance to hear further details about the visitor, fearing his wife would supply information he'd rather not know. But Melanie persisted.

"He said his name is Daniel Merriman," she continued, and gave a description of his appearance.

Fear rippled through Gareth. Surely not? It was impossible. He'd satisfied himself it was an illusion he'd seen on the beach. Daniel Merriman was dead. Died about a decade ago in that incident.

"Is there something wrong?" Melanie could see he'd grown tensely rigid, now sitting upright on the sofa.

"Just tired from the day," he replied. While partly true, it was the naming of the mystery man that set his nerves on edge again.

"Have you ever heard of him?" Melanie sat on the sofa beside him, placing a comforting arm round his shoulders.

"No," Gareth lied. Of course he'd heard of him. Had known him well.

"It must be some weirdo trying to scam us into believing he's an old friend, for a reason beyond my comprehension," Gareth continued his deception. "I'll sort out getting the door locks changed, get CCTV to monitor the outside, and install a security alarm," he promised, reassuring her.

Melanie nodded approval at the same moment the door-bell rang.

"That must be your pizza delivery," she said, leaving to answer the door.

Gareth remained on the sofa. Someone, he thought, must be playing a sick joke. His wife's description of the intruder matched the person he'd known. The same as he'd seen on holiday. They'd worked together as accountants for the same company around a decade ago, not long before he married. It had to be an impostor. Daniel Merriman was dead. Of that he was certain.

CHAPTER 4

GARETH remained embroiled at work in meetings about the possible merger of his company, often working late.

Each evening he returned home exhausted, and was glad when the weekend arrived. Melanie's workload had also increased during the week, and she was also relieved to have the break. More time for recreation.

The stranger who'd entered the house had creeped her out. But now with the door locks changed and someone coming to install CCTV next week, she felt more secure.

She decided the weirdo had seen her social media posts and gleaned some knowledge about her and the family from them, so now restricted them to just friends.

Melanie enjoyed water colour painting, and was presently putting the finishing touches to a seascape, working from a photo taken while on their holiday. An easel erected in a small room upstairs served as her art studio. Gareth was seated on the sofa in the living room watching afternoon sport on TV.

There had been no more unwelcome visits from the man purporting to be Daniel Merriman, and the trauma of his intrusion, it seemed, was now over.

"There's a man in the garden watching us play catch with our ball," said Amelia, entering the living room. Gareth muted the TV.

"What?" he turned to her looking alarmed.

"We were playing catch, when Sophie saw him standing there, smiling at us."

Gareth shot up from the sofa and headed for the kitchen back door, his daughter following. He was met by Amelia about to come in.

"Where's the man?" he asked rushing into the garden and surveilling the lawn containing an apple tree and shed on the left side and flower bed on the right. He could see no-one in the fenced enclosure.

"He was here daddy," the children insisted, fearing their father might think they were playing a trick on him.

"What's happening?" Melanie now joined them after hearing raised voices through the upstairs window.

"The girls said there was a man here just now, watching them play a ball game," Gareth explained. Melanie's face registered dread. Quickly she placed her protective arms around the children.

"I'll check the shed," Gareth strode decisively towards it, flinging open the door, his adrenalin surged ready to take on any attack from an intruder hiding inside.

A mower, shelves and hooks for garden equipment, a rolled up rug, pine cabinet, deckchairs and a variety of other items took up much of the room. An intruder would be hard pressed to effectively hide in there.

"What did he look like?" he asked the youngsters. They weren't sure about a full description because his appearance had taken them by surprise. But the one Sophie recalled of black jeans, open neck blue shirt and brown swept back hair, was enough for Melanie's dread to become reinforced.

"Let's call the police," Melanie insisted, after telling the youngsters to go inside the house.

"Do you think we should?" Gareth hesitated. "There's nothing to suggest anyone was here. Perhaps the children made it up. He'd have needed to climb over the fences of several neighbours to get in. It's unlikely isn't it?"

"But they described the same person I saw the other day, explain that?" Melanie quizzed. "I never told the girls what he looked like." She was puzzled by her husband's reluctance.

"I suppose you're right," he conceded. While he would do everything to make sure his wife and children were safe, he was terrified of the horrific past at Falcombe Sands descending on his life again.

****

A POLICE officer called next day after Melanie had contacted them. She advised on security for the house, which was generally good already. The CCTV installation to come ticked another box, and new window and door locks were commended.

The officer mildly reprimanded Melanie for not putting on the security alarm the day she returned to the house to find the stranger inside. Melanie had already reprimanded herself for the oversight many times since.

Taking a description of the intruder, the officer left promising to instigate a search bulletin for patrols in the area, and to conduct a check for anyone living in the locality who might have a similar history of impersonation like the man calling himself Daniel Merriman.

For the next few weeks the unwelcome visitor made no appearance. And with the extra security and CCTV now installed, Melanie felt the house well covered. Gareth also began to relax again. Tension, brought on by the inexplicable appearances, had caused him to develop an unusually short fuse with his family over the merest annoyance. Now he'd settled back into familiar grumbling.

The household seemed restored to normal, until one day Melanie was called away from home working to attend a meeting in the office. Travelling by underground train in order to avoid inner London traffic jams, the return journey was delayed due to a problem on the line. She'd planned to get home in time to make the ten minute drive to collect the children from school, but was now running late.

When she arrived, a woman stood with her young son by the school gate entrance. Both women had grown to know each other fairly well, waiting daily for the children to finish their last lesson. Usually buzzing with end of day excitement among the youngsters, the playground was now empty.

"I saw you hadn't arrived, so I looked after Amelia and Sophie while we waited," the woman explained, smiling from her friendly face. "A man arrived to say you'd asked him to collect them for you, as you were running late. Said his name was Daniel."

Panic gripped Melanie, her gaping eyes revealing the terror inside.

"Are you okay?" the woman began to feel Melanie's fear. "Should I have stopped him? He seemed genuine, knowing your name, that you were running late."

Melanie hardly heard the woman's words, thoughts of the children coming to dreadful harm or being stolen clouded her mind.

"He said he was going to take them to the local park," the parent's words filtered into Melanie's mind. The urgent need to check it out drove her into action. She was off, leaving the messenger troubled and confused.

The park was a five-minute walk away, which Melanie ran in less than two. When she arrived, the greatest sense of relief she had ever felt coursed through her, seeing Sophie and Amelia excitedly chattering to each other swaying back and forth on the swings. Their mother approached, emotions of terror and joy swilling erratically inside.

"What the hell are you doing coming here with a complete stranger? I've warned you so many times not to go off with anyone you don't know."

The girls expressions changed from carefree to misery in seconds, fearing mother's wrath. Their faces creased and teardrops began to trickle down their cheeks.

"Oh come here, I'm so sorry. I didn't mean to upset you." Melanie opened her arms as the youngsters dismounted the swings to be embraced by her. Now tears began to well in her eyes.

"We're sorry mum," said Amelia, "but that man who was in our garden the other week said he knew you."

"Yes, he told us you'd asked him to collect us from school because you'd be late," added Sophie.

"He's over there on the bench," Amelia pointed, but the bench was empty.

****

GARETH had hardly entered the front door from work when Melanie began recounting the event.

"Do you know who this person, this weirdo is? You get very edgy whenever he's mentioned or made an appearance," she challenged him to tell her all he knew.

"I've absolutely no idea who he is," Gareth responded, taking off his jacket. "It worries me just like it does you. That's why I seem edgy." His reply did not sound convincing to Melanie.

"I've called the police. They suggest we keep the girls at home for a few days while they make more enquiries," she told him, as he made his way into the living room, placing his jacket over the back of a chair and opening the drinks cabinet to pour himself a whisky.

"You're starting a bit early," Melanie frowned. "Can't you wait until after dinner?"

"Stop stressing me out!" Gareth shouted, downing the drink in a couple of gulps.

"I'm stressed out too, worrying about the children's safety," Melanie returned equally.

"What do you want me to do then, chain them and lock them in their rooms?" Gareth's face turned deep red, inflamed with fury. He poured another whisky, his hands starting to shake.

"Do you know this man?" Melanie fired the question at him again.

"Of course not," Gareth stared at her in amazement. "Why on earth would you think that?"

Her eyes searched the puzzled reaction in his expression. Still she wasn't entirely convinced by his response. Ever since the appearance of Daniel Merriman, her husband had become rattled. But not just because he feared for the safety of his family. She felt sure something in the past had happened between them, causing him to grow on edge. It was a sheer guess, but calculated on intuition.

As advised by the police, Melanie kept the children at home for the next few days, but knew that it would only offer temporary protection. Patrols and a search through police records for criminals matching the description of Daniel Merriman hadn't found any likely candidates.

On Saturday the family went out for an early evening meal at a local Chinese restaurant that always served delicious food. The setting was busy with waiters weaving from table to table in the capacious room filled almost to capacity with diners.

The family was guided to seating beside a colourful tropical fish aquarium containing among its submerged decorations an ornamental bridge, a miniature sunken ship, small rocks and pebbles. Air bubbles rose to the top at one side in a continuous stream.

"Look there's an angel fish," said Sophie, pointing excitedly as she settled on a seat.

"And some guppies," Amelia joined in.

"What's that one?" Melanie asked them, indicating a fish that was hovering with an inquisitive stare through the glass.

"A goldfish," ventured Sophie.

"No, goldfish are an orangey gold colour," Melanie corrected, "you know that." The youngster looked deflated. "It's a catfish," her mother smiled, not wishing the girl to be unhappy.

"Oh yes, I meant to say that," Sophie told a little white lie.

A few minutes later a waiter arrived to take their orders. General chat followed about what the girls had done at school when they'd returned from their few days stay at home, and they were particularly enthusiastic talking of a school coach outing to an activity centre in the coming week.

"Are you okay?" Melanie asked Gareth, noticing his attention seemed to be distracted in deep thought, only nodding and smiling distantly to give the appearance of hearing their conversation.

"No, I'm fine," he gave another smile. "Just been a pressured week at work. Takes a little time to unload."

Melanie was not fooled by his response, but didn't want to take issue with it and spoil the evening. The waiter returned a short time later to serve the family's meals, and chatter largely fell silent to concentrate on enjoying the food.

Then Melanie noticed Gareth glancing past Sophie, sitting opposite at the table, towards the glass swing door entrance about twenty feet away. His expression changed from searching curiosity to a look of gaping disbelief.

"What's the matter?" she asked, sounding alarmed and turning to see what had caught his attention. She could see no-one entering the restaurant or in the aisle. Gareth made no reply, just staring transfixed.

"What's the matter daddy?" the children had noticed his strange expression.

Gareth hadn't heard his wife or the youngsters. All he could see was Daniel Merriman approaching the table.

"Hello," the arrival greeted him. "A Chinese meal, how lucky you and your family are. I used to enjoy those once." He glanced at the array of meals, sweet and sour chicken, satay prawns, vegetable spring rolls, noodles, mushrooms among the selection.

"You're dead, I'm imagining you," Gareth mumbled, panic rising in his wavering voice.

"You're right, my old friend, on the dead part. But you're certainly not imagining me," Daniel smiled. "Just thought I'd join you for a while."

"Gareth, who are you talking to?" Melanie broke in. He didn't hear her.

"What's the matter with daddy?" the girls had stopped eating, deep concern registering on their faces. Like Melanie, they couldn't see or hear who their father was speaking with.

"Must be wonderful to have a family and spend time playing games with your daughters, and have such a beautiful wife," Daniel continued. "I would love to have had my own family, but of course, you put a stop to that."

Gareth rose from his chair.

"Get out!" he shouted. "You can't exist."

"But I do, as you can see. No-one else in the restaurant including your family can see or hear me, so you're making a complete spectacle of yourself in front of everyone." Daniel smiled again.

"For God's sake sit down, pull yourself together," now Melanie's temper flew. The diners had all stopped eating, eyes fixed on the scene of the outburst.

"Anyway, enjoy your outing," Daniel gave his good wishes and disappeared.

"Is there something wrong?" a dark suited man, who Melanie took to be the manager, came to the table.

"No, it's okay," she assured him. "My husband has been overwrought lately. Everything's fine now." Her embarrassment was visible in her reddened complexion. Gareth sat down, staring blankly ahead.

"Daddy, aren't you feeling well?" Amelia appeared fearful. Gareth was lost in his thoughts, unaware of his surroundings.

"I think we'd better get daddy home. He's just very tired," Melanie did her best to reassure the children, and asked for the bill.

CHAPTER 5

ON their return home, Melanie settled the girls to bed, though she wasn't sure they'd rest well. Her repeated attempts to tell them their father would be better after a night's sleep didn't remove the troubled frowns.

When Melanie went downstairs to ask Gareth about his outburst in the restaurant, he was leaning forward on the sofa with a bottle of whisky on the small table in front of him, and a glass of it in his hand. For a moment she stood taking in his fretful appearance.

"You seemed to be talking to someone in the restaurant, getting upset. None of us could see who it was." Melanie hoped to coax some rational explanation for his behaviour. Gareth didn't reply, and took a swig of whisky.

"Perhaps you're overworking. Maybe you should take some time off work. Relax for a while."

Gareth continued to ignore her advice.

"The children are very worried about you. It would help if you spoke to them tomorrow. Assure them that you've just had a pressured time at work, but everything's settled now," Melanie suggested a way he could stop the girls worrying. Gareth turned his head to face her.

"For Christ's sake, I am under great pressure, but it has nothing to do with work," he shouted, almost on the point of telling her what was troubling him. But he couldn't bring himself to confess.

"Tell me what it is," Melanie insisted. He didn't respond, and unscrewed the cap of the whisky bottle to top up his glass with a large serving.

"Just leave me alone," he said, and downed a generous gulp.

"I'm going to bed," Melanie turned and left, knowing she would get no further with him for now.

****

THE following day Gareth had recovered a little from his shell like state and took the youngsters for their promised visit to the local play centre. Melanie drove over to see her widowed mother, Evelyn, living five miles away.

"I've just put the kettle on," came the greeting as she entered the house. "Go and make yourself comfortable in the sitting room," her mother suggested with a welcoming wrinkled smile, while lightly touching her grey hair curls to make sure they were neatly in place.

"Is that new?" asked Melanie, noting her blue ankle length herringbone dress.

"Yes, bought it yesterday. Do you like it?"

Melanie nodded approval, then entered the sitting room, settling on a fabric olive sofa. She surveyed the familiar floral wallpaper, electric fire, glass cabinet containing decorative china, and shelves with miniature plaster rabbits playing musical instruments.

Soon Evelyn came in carrying a tray with tea and biscuits, placing it on a side table and sitting down beside her daughter. They chatted about the weather, a new coat her mother had also bought recently, and the children.

The subject of the youngsters brought Melanie to her concerns about Gareth.

"I've never liked him," Evelyn voiced her often repeated opinion of her daughter's husband, after hearing of his latest strange behaviour. "Something about him. As if he's carrying some shady secret."

"Mum, he's a good man," Melanie defended him. "A good husband and father. But ever since this stranger appeared he's become different."

"Like I say, he's hiding some shady secret. Seems to me this person who's showed up has got something on him." Evelyn began eating a chocolate biscuit. Melanie sipped her tea.

"I've always thought the man who came here a few times with you and Gareth, before you got married, was a much nicer person." Evelyn voiced another opinion, pausing halfway through the biscuit. She was never short of an opinion. "I struggle to remember his name, but he'd have made a much better husband for you."

"I've absolutely no idea who you're talking about," Melanie shook her head.

"What was his name?" Evelyn pondered, not listening to her daughter's reply, too absorbed in trying to remember. She topped up their teacups, reciting different names under her breath, but reaching no definite recollection.

"Tell me the name again of this person who's been troubling you?" her mother asked.

"Daniel Merriman," said Melanie, repeating what she'd already told her mother some days earlier.

"I don't know why, but something seems to ring a bell with that name. I just can't put my finger on it," Evelyn gazed perplexed. "My memory, sorry to say, isn't what it was." Both women fell silent for a moment.

"Have you ever thought of leaving him?" Evelyn didn't dress up the question.

"Gareth?" Melanie was shocked by the suggestion. "No I have not!" she replied angrily. "He's just having a difficult time right now."

Her mother realised she'd breached the barrier of tact and dropped the subject for the time being. Their chat returned to everyday matters, rising prices for food, Melanie's work, and local gossip Evelyn had heard from her neighbourhood friends.

On the drive back home Melanie couldn't help hearing her mother's words 'shady secret' repeating in her mind. Is that why Gareth is behaving so oddly she wondered? Did this Merriman stranger have some hold over him? Did Gareth owe him money? Was the stranger blackmailing him over some mistake Gareth had made in the past? Perhaps she could persuade him to tell her all. Maybe she could help if he did. Probably the time wasn't yet right though to coax it out of him.

CHAPTER 6

WHEN Melanie returned to the house she could hear the girls through the open kitchen door playing excitedly in the garden.

"You dropped it," shouted Amelia.

"No I didn't. I caught the ball, then I dropped it," Sophie objected.

"I'm back," their mother called to them. The youngsters stopped their game and came inside.

"Did you have a good time at the play centre?" Melanie asked, putting the kettle on.

"There's a new climbing frame," Amelia announced.

"I climbed it faster than Amelia," Sophie piped in.

"No you didn't," her sister insisted.

"Okay, stop arguing girls," Melanie ordered. "Where's your dad?"

"He's in the living room," they replied. A loaded silence fell between them for a moment.

"I think daddy still isn't feeling very well," Sophie said, the glow of her upbeat mood fading.

"What do you mean?" Melanie grew concerned.

"While we were playing, we saw him looking unhappy," the girl glanced at her sister, whose sad face confirmed her description.

"He looked sometimes like he was talking to himself," Sophie continued.

"And he didn't say anything to us when we were walking back home," Amelia added.

"Alright, you go and play in the garden again while I see your daddy," Melanie directed. The girls returned to the garden while their mother entered the living room.

Gareth sat on the sofa, a tumbler and a bottle of whisky on the small table beside.

"You don't usually drink this early," she said to him. "I wish you would tell me what is troubling you."

Gareth picked up the tumbler and took a swig of the spirit, then replaced the glass on the table. He continued to stare ahead as if in a trance, seeming not to hear his wife or acknowledge she'd entered the room.

Melanie sat on the sofa beside him.

"Perhaps you ought to see the doctor," she suggested softly. "Take a week off work. A good rest will help a lot."

For the first time he reacted to her presence, turning his head to look at her for a moment with an expression of contempt.

"You couldn't do a thing about it if I told you. Nor could a doctor, a head shrink, or the winner of the brightest brain in the world contest," Gareth delivered his verdict and resumed staring blankly ahead.

The wall he'd built around himself could not yet be breached, Melanie concluded. She sat beside him for a while longer, hoping he might relent and tell all, then rose and left the room.

****

40

LATER that day Melanie was dishing dinner on to plates as the girls arrived from freshening up for the meal.

"Sophie, go and tell daddy his dinner's ready," she said. "Amelia go and set the table in the dining room." Sophie returned from the living room after a few moments.

"Daddy doesn't want any dinner. He says he's going to bed," she announced. Melanie's concern for her husband grew deeper, but she hid her feelings not wanting to worry the youngsters further about his strange behaviour.

After dinner she settled the girls to bed with a story, then went downstairs to watch television for a while on her own. She hoped it might provide a temporary distraction from the concerns playing on her mind, but the characters on screen seemed to be hazily talking and acting a million miles away.

She desperately tried to work out why her husband was so troubled. It had all begun when they were on holiday at Falcombe Sands. He'd been reluctant to go there. Why? Had something happened there in the past? What? How could she know without him telling? She turned off the TV and made her way up to bed.

Gareth was snoring. At least he was getting some rest. Probably with the help of the whisky, she thought. Climbing in beside him, Melanie lay there, her worries and the snoring not aiding her rest. Eventually she slipped into sleep.

****

LOUD music shook the room. Couples dancing, their smiles and eyes fixed in magnetic attraction to each other. More partygoers stood chatting and drinking at the side.

Melanie caught the glance of a man who looked like the Daniel Merriman who'd appeared in her house. He was dressed in a light blue, short sleeved shirt and dark trousers, and had been talking to a group of friends.

For a moment they stared at each other, and the swell of the room seemed to fade away. He began to zigzag between the dancers moving towards her, nearing as if he was intending to ask her to dance. Next moment he began to dissolve, his body disintegrating into a skeleton.

Melanie awoke in terror, sweat pouring out. She sat bolt upright in bed. Gareth stopped snoring, mumbling displeasure, then turned and resumed snoring. Melanie remained sitting up, the impact of the nightmare slowly beginning to lessen. But the image of Merriman's horrific transformation was still vivid. What the hell was that about? Had she actually met this man before? Or was his appearance in the house now playing on her mind in the most bizarre way?

For a long time she continued to sit up, puzzling at the reason for the terrifying dream. She feared sleeping again in case the nightmare returned. Gradually she settled into a fitful rest.

CHAPTER 7

GARETH sat in his office studying account figures on the desk screen. His phone rang.

"There's a man in reception asking to see you," came the voice. "Says it's an important matter."

"Who is it?" Gareth asked.

"Won't say. Says he needs to speak to you personally."

"Okay, I'll come down," Gareth replied grudgingly.

He stepped out of the lift into the large glass fronted reception area with tall pot plants, seating and magazines on a long table, and glanced at the desk to see neither the receptionist behind it or any visitor waiting beside it.

A man sat on one of the chairs and Gareth approached, introducing himself and asking if he was the person calling on him. The man shook his head.

At that moment the receptionist appeared from a door behind the desk.

"Joanna, where's the person who wanted to see me?" he asked

"Sorry, I was called away," the smartly dressed young woman in a navy trouser suit apologised for her temporary absence.

"That's okay. But do you know if my caller has left?" Gareth looked around again, checking he hadn't missed sight of the visitor.

"I can't be sure, but it looks like he has," Joanna surveyed the reception area, still feeling apologetic over not being present for a few minutes.

"Not to worry," Gareth smiled, hiding annoyance at being disturbed for no reason. He walked towards the lift, then thought to ask Joanna if she could describe the mystery man. Turning back to reception, he saw another visitor had entered the building and the receptionist was now busy talking to her. He decided to leave it.

On the way back, he stopped to take a drink from the water dispenser in the corridor close to his office, then entered the room.

Sitting in his chair was Daniel Merriman. Gareth stood rigid, a blast of adrenalin urged him to take flight. But his body felt clamped to the spot.

"Don't take on so old friend," Daniel grinned, detecting his terror. "I thought you'd be glad to see me again. Have a chat."

"Are you still alive?" Gareth struggled to ask.

"Now what a silly question," Daniel replied patronisingly.

"I saw them bury you. I was at your funeral." The vision of the ceremony came flooding back to Gareth, though seeing the figure in front of him made him doubt his senses.

"Yes, I am dead," Merriman leaned back in the chair, nestling his hands behind his head. "So it can only lead to one conclusion that I'm a ghost."

Gareth stepped back in shock, hearing confirmation of his fear. Slowly he regained some composure.

"No, you're not a ghost," he snarled. "It's a trick. You're a lookalike, an identical twin of Daniel I never knew about, or just my imagination."

Daniel instantly disappeared.

A few minutes passed, and after pacing the office in thought, Gareth concluded it was his revisiting Falcombe Sands on holiday, that must have sparked a vivid memory centre in his brain of that dire past event, causing him to hallucinate. He needed rest as his wife had prescribed. The explanation began to settle him, then Daniel reappeared on the chair.

"Convinced now I'm a ghost?" he smiled.

Sweat began to pour from Gareth. There truly was no escape from this nightmare.

"There's a bit of a score to settle, isn't there my old friend?" the ghost declared. "You know what it's for."

"I'll have you exorcised," Gareth threatened.

"Oh, some mumbo jumbo ceremony. I think that belongs to the Middle Ages, don't you old friend?" Daniel derided the suggestion.

His old friend now stood rigidly still again, trying to think of a way to escape this terrifying situation.

The spirit unfolded his hands from behind his head and leaned forward in the chair, resting his arms on the desk.

"You are so lucky. You have a wonderful family. Such a good looking, clever wife and lovely daughters. I think Amelia and Sophie had a great time when I took them to the park," Daniel reflected.

"Leave my children alone. You've no right to interfere in their lives. I don't want them frightened," Gareth responded angrily.

"I apologise if I've frightened them," the ghost replied calmly. "It's never been my intention, and they didn't seem frightened when I appeared in your garden, and when we visited the park."

"I don't care. Just leave them alone. And my wife." Gareth's anger remained unabated. "And you can bloody well leave me alone too. Just go to hell."

Daniel studied him silently, noting the bulging fury in his old friend's eyes.

"I don't think it will be me going to hell Gareth," the spirit pointedly remarked. "And by the way, I see you've grown a beard since our earlier days together. Suits you. Gives you a look of maturity and wisdom."

Gareth turned sharply, alarmed by loud knocking at the door. It opened and a middle-aged woman peered in, wearing a grey trouser suit, white shirt and pink rimmed spectacles.

"Is all well?" she enquired. "I thought I heard shouting in here as I came down the corridor."

Gareth looked at her sheepishly.

"Y…yes Beverly," he muttered, feeling foolish.

The woman gazed round the office, noting there was no-one else present.

"Good. Just thought I ought to check," she said, eyeing him curiously, wondering why he was denying the shouting she had definitely heard coming from the room.

****

EVELYN leaned forward, handing beakers of lemonade to her grandchildren Amelia and Sophie.

"Did you enjoy the cakes?" she asked. "Yes," the girls replied in unison, hoping they might get another before leaving.

"It's lovely to see you both. Your mother doesn't bring you to visit me half as often as I'd like," she told them, with the barb indirectly aimed at Melanie standing beside her in the kitchen.

"We're on our half term break," Amelia told her, "and mummy's promised to take us to see a film this afternoon called Pavlo's Great Escape."

"It's about a silly dog who's always getting into trouble," Sophie added excitedly.

"Is that right?" their grandmother smiled. "You're very lucky girls." The youngsters nodded agreement.

"Now your mother and I are going to have a little chat, so why don't you take your drinks into the garden and play for a while," Evelyn suggested. The girls nodded again and made their way to the hall back door leading to the garden. Melanie and her mother settled on the sitting room sofa with cups of tea on the small table in front of them.

"I can tell you're troubled," Evelyn opened the chat. Melanie looked down for a moment, reflecting on her troubles.

"Gareth seems to be lost in his thoughts much of the time. He loses his temper frequently, even throws things around," she poured out her desperation. "I'm worried he might even become violent."

Evelyn shook her head.

"I told you I never liked him," she said, worried for her daughter and the girls, and satisfied her long held judgement about him appeared to be correct.

"But it isn't like Gareth. He's always been a very good father and husband, until this person from his past suddenly came on to the scene," Melanie defended.

"Well it seems to me there must be some murky past. That this person has some hold over him. I've told you before." Evelyn lifted her teacup, taking a drink.

"Have you asked him to tell you about this er…what's his name?" she continued.

"Daniel Merriman. Yes, of course I have, many times. But Gareth gets angry, then shuts down for hours," Melanie grew distressed.

"Then you should seriously consider leaving him," Evelyn began again. "Stay here with the children, at least for a while. I've got room for you all."

"I think that will make him even worse," Melanie didn't consider it a good idea. "And the children would be even more unsettled suddenly taken from their home. I've got to try and get through to him." Despite turning down the idea, Melanie did feel torn between two options.

"Well alright," her mother accepted grudgingly. "But I think you and the children would be better off getting out."

This time the conversation had become too serious to move on to other matters.

"It's not long before the girls' film starts," Melanie began to rise from the sofa.

"You haven't touched your tea," Evelyn glanced at the cup. "You've hardly spent any time here."

"Sorry, next time." Melanie went to the back door to call in the youngsters. She didn't want to stay and discuss it any longer. The choice between staying with Gareth or leaving was becoming too painful.

"I'll see you again soon," she told her mother, who'd joined her in the hall to say goodbye.

When they'd left, Evelyn wrestled for an idea that could separate her daughter and the girls from Gareth. She feared he might go on to cause them harm. Several times she considered making a phone call.

CHAPTER 8

NEXT morning Gareth stood by the living room door saying goodbye to the children as he prepared to leave for work. They were watching a cartoon on the TV and glanced across from the sofa, raising their hands in reply.

As he approached the front door the doorbell rang. Opening it he saw two uniformed police officers, a man and woman, standing there.

"Good morning sir," the man said.

"Is there something wrong?" Gareth asked, surprised to see them.

"I'm Constable Roger Hutton, and this is Constable Carole Mahoney," he nodded toward his colleague. "May we come in sir?"

"Well I'm just off to work…"

"We hope it won't take long," the woman cut in.

"I hope not," Gareth replied testily.

The officers stepped inside, just as Melanie entered the hall.

"What's wrong?" she asked, looking worried.

"It's okay madam," Constable Mahoney assured, "just paying a call."

"A call for what?" her concern wasn't allayed.

"May we go inside?"

"The children are in the living room watching television. I don't want to worry them," Melanie pleaded protectively. "Can we talk in the kitchen?"

The officers agreed.

"I'll take a look in on the children," said WPC Mahoney, making for the sound of the TV.

Used cups, plates and cereal bowls were spread on the kitchen counter. Melanie indicated a chair at the table for him to sit.

"No, it's alright madam, I'd prefer to stand," PC Hutton declined.

"What is this all about?" Gareth was growing impatient, scowling at the policeman.

"We've had a report from someone who's concerned that there's been antisocial behaviour here," he said.

"What!" Melanie and Gareth stiffened in shock.

"Who reported it?" Gareth growled.

"I'm not at liberty to say, sir," the officer replied.

"This is outrageous," now Gareth was furious.

"We just want to take a look around. No need to get upset." The policeman's calm response infuriated Gareth even more, but Melanie grabbed his arm to make him keep his composure.

"I know who did this," Gareth mouthed between his clenched teeth.

In the living room WPC Mahoney spoke to the youngsters.

"Good cartoon?" she asked, attempting to make them feel at ease with their surprise visitor.

"The pirates from space are trying to steal a magic necklace," explained Sophie enthusiastically.

"No, it's a magic amulet," her sister corrected.

"Sounds amazing," the officer enthused.

51

"Why are you here?" Amelia enquired, puzzled by the stranger. "Have mummy and daddy done something wrong?"

"Of course not," she assured them. "We're just having a little chat. There's nothing to worry about."

The youngsters seemed satisfied with the reply, and resumed watching the cartoon.

"We'd like to take a look around upstairs," said PC Hutton, when his colleague returned.

"If you must," Gareth gnarled his teeth.

"This is your bloody mother's doing, isn't?" he accused, when the officer's had left the kitchen. "She's always done her bloody best to separate us. But this is too far."

"We don't know it was her," Melanie tried to calm him.

"Well who else do you think it was, a Norwegian fisherman?"

"Don't be ridiculous," now Melanie was growing angry. "I'm going to see the children."

"A few minutes later the officers came downstairs. Melanie returned from the living room, relieved that the youngsters weren't worried about the 'nice police lady'.

"Well thank you for your time," said the WPC as her colleague cast a final eye round the kitchen.

"Everything's alright isn't it?" Melanie's concern about their visit hadn't diminished.

"We appreciate your co-operation," came the non committal reply from PC Hutton.

After they'd left, Gareth tapped a number on his phone.

"What are you doing?"

Her husband ignored her.

"Hello," Evelyn answered the call.

"It was you wasn't it?" Gareth shouted.

"What?"

Gareth hung up, a confused expression forming on his face. New dread gripped him. Was it that bloody Merriman who'd called the police? Could a ghost do that? A ghost could probably do anything he concluded. Gareth's anger began turning to fear.

"Are you okay?" Melanie saw him paling. He said nothing, making his way to the front door and leaving. A few minutes later Melanie's phone rang.

"That was your husband shouting at me, wasn't it," Evelyn sounded upset. Her daughter couldn't deny it.

"He's just a bit worked up, that's all," Melanie attempted to defuse the situation.

"What is he accusing me of?" her mother insisted.

Melanie hesitated over giving the explanation, but relented.

"I've certainly thought about calling the police," Evelyn admitted, after her daughter described what had happened.

"Did you do it?" Melanie probed. This time her mother hesitated.

"I picked up the phone," she paused, "but I put it down again."

Both women were silent for a moment, daughter wondering if it was the whole truth, and Evelyn unsure if she was believed.

"I hope you didn't," Melanie replied gravely. "I've enough to contend with at the minute, without the police alerting social services and wanting to take the children away."

If her mother was telling the truth, it left Melanie with the question of who did phone the police?

****

GARETH entered the house after work. The silence struck him. Usually he could hear the children's voices in the living room, sometimes talking upstairs, or playing in the garden."

"Melanie?" he called from the hallway. No response. He checked the rooms. All were empty. Placing his jacket over a chair in the kitchen he rang his wife.

"Where are you all?" he asked, anticipating she'd taken them to the local park, or was giving them a treat somewhere. For a moment she didn't answer.

"I'm at my mother's," her voice wavered.

"Just visiting?" he ventured. Melanie remained silent again for several seconds.

"I think it's best if I stayed here with the children for a little while. Put a bit of space between us and let things settle for a few days or so."

"What?" Gareth exploded furiously.

"Amelia and Sophie are worried about you. Your moods are upsetting them," Melanie gave a faltering explanation. "I've said you need some peace for a while, sorting out a few problems. They said they'd enjoy a few days stay at their grandma's."

"That bloody witch interfering again is she?" Gareth ended the call.

Half-an-hour later he parked on the road outside Evelyn's house, got out the car and stormed down the front garden path, knocking heavily on her door and repeatedly ringing the doorbell.

There was no response at first, then Evelyn cautiously opened up with the security chain in place.

"Open up you damned troublemaker," Gareth shouted.

"Go away," his mother-in-law ordered. "You're frightening your wife and children."

Gareth calmed a little, not wishing to cause them any upset.

"Let me talk to my wife," he demanded.

"She doesn't want to talk to you. Now go away, or I'll call the police."

"It's okay mum," Melanie interrupted, slipping the security chain off and opening the door.

"What the hell are you doing?" Gareth demanded in desperation.

"I think it's just best for us all at the minute. You need to work through your difficulties. You're upsetting the children and me with your strange behaviour," Melanie's stress poured out. "I've offered to try and help, but you just shut me out."

Gareth's pent up fury faltered. How in God's name could he tell her a ghost from the past was haunting him. He'd be certified insane.

"I wish you'd come home," he pleaded.

"Is that daddy?" Amelia came to the door with Sophie following.

"Hello my lovelies," their father smiled.

"We're staying with grandma for a few days," Sophie edged to stand beside her sister. "She's promised to buy us some new toys as a half term present."

"She has, has she?" Gareth replied cynically. He realised for now his mother-in-law held the trump card. Any further action on his part could worsen the situation. It required some thought.

"Come home soon," he said to Melanie, who now stood behind the children. A teardrop trickled from her left eye, which she hurriedly wiped away with her hand. Gareth said goodbye to the children and returned to the car.

CHAPTER 9

BACK home, Gareth took a bottle of whisky from the drinks cabinet in the living room and poured a drink. Then he went to the kitchen and took a shepherd's pie ready meal from the fridge, heating it in the microwave.

Sitting at the kitchen table with the food and glass of whisky, he stabbed half-heartedly at the meal with a fork, but abandoned it halfway in preference to consuming alcohol.

Returning to the living room, he switched on the TV and settled on the sofa. The house makeover programme remained a distant haze of sound and movement, as his woes took centre stage. The lack of activity in the home added to his all consuming solitude. Only whisky helped anaesthetize the anguish.

After a while, his eyes swam in and out of focus. Rising unsteadily to his feet, he swayed his way upstairs to the bedroom. Fully clothed, he collapsed on the bed and faded into sleep.

In the early hours he woke, sensing he was not alone. His head throbbed painfully, his mouth bone dry. For a few seconds hope that Melanie had returned and was present reduced the unpleasant effects of a hangover, until he heard a voice.

"Been overdoing the ol' devil juice have we?" Daniel Merriman joked. "You're older now than when we used to knock it back a bit. Have to pace yourself better these days."

Gareth hoisted himself up on the bed, seeing in the darkness his tormentor's illuminated spirit body seated on the dressing table chair.

"For heaven's sake just go away, leave me alone," Gareth pleaded. Daniel ignored the plea.

"Things not going so well for you old friend?"

"No they're bloody not, because of you," shouted Gareth, then winced as the loud sound of his own voice sent a shot of pain through his head.

"Calm yourself," Daniel replied, smiling. "You'll give yourself a headache."

"It was you who made that call to the police, wasn't it?" Gareth accused.

"Maybe, maybe not. It could have been your mother-in-law. You're not exactly her flavour of the month."

At that moment Gareth's phone began ringing downstairs. New hope it could be his wife made him leap from the bed and quickly make his way downstairs to pick it up from kitchen counter.

"Melanie?" he asked eagerly. There came no reply. "Melanie, is it you?" The line went dead. He checked to see the last call number. It read withheld.

Downhearted, he made his way wearily upstairs to the bedroom. Daniel Merriman was gone. Gareth slumped back on the bed, his mind wrestling with an idea to rid himself of visitations from his former friend.

Finding a priest who performed exorcisms might be a possible solution came to mind. But first he'd have to find one, and it wasn't exactly a modern belief these days. Daniel had been a wily person in life, and Gareth feared he'd be one step ahead in the afterlife of avoiding any religious incantation. It could even antagonise the spirit and make the hauntings worse.

Gareth wondered if a graveside vow of repentance for his wrongdoing might lead his former friend to settle the matter. Yes, that could be the answer. Although not entirely convinced it would provide the solution, he rested a little more easily. That is, until a nightmare in his restless slumber re-enacted the scene of the damning event at Falcombe Sands.

****

GARETH still suffered a headache from his excessive drinking the previous night, as he drove on the two hour journey to Cattleford, a rural village in West Sussex.

The country view on route of hills and pastures as he neared his destination, helped to refresh his mind and ease the throbbing headache.

The village high street with a minimart, grocery store, newsagent, post office and inn, seemed a far cry from his overcrowded London home setting. Grey stone cottages interspersed the shops and lined side roads, lending an air of age old stability.

The spire of St Peter's Church, where he was heading, could be seen rising behind the properties, making the side turn ahead an obvious signpost towards it.

Parking on the road outside, Gareth made his way through the lych gate into the graveyard. Headstones weathered by time and patches of yellowing lichen, featured the names of dearly departed, the inscriptions now worn down and almost unreadable through the ravages of time.

He moved on to a headstone situated in a section devoted to less ancient burials, and stopped to read the dedication engraved on it. 'Our dearly loved son Daniel William Merriman returned to God in his 34th year'.

Gareth stood praying for forgiveness, guiltily recalling the incident that had brought about this interment. As he prayed, he became aware of being approached. He turned see an elderly grey-haired man in a dark suit, accompanied by a woman of similar years wearing a black dress and pill box hat. She held a bunch of flowers.

"If I'm not mistaken, it's Gareth," said the man with a smile creasing the lines in his round, healthy face. "How wonderful to see you," he shook Gareth's hand.

"It's been a long time since we last met," the woman greeted warmly.

"Hello Roy and Hilda," Gareth did his best to reciprocate a friendly welcome to Daniel's parents, while his sense of guilt deepened that their son lay buried there because of him.

"What brings you here today?" Roy asked.

"I have some time off work, and I thought I'd drive over and pay my respects to my dear friend." Gareth had to think of a reason swiftly, and thought it sounded a bit hollow, as it was the first time he'd been here since Daniel's funeral, and the last occasion when he'd met them. But the couple accepted his explanation without further question.

"If only we'd known you were coming we could have arranged for you to stay overnight with us and talked about the times you shared with Daniel," said Roy. "We know you were both very close."

"Sorry, I didn't want to impose on you," Gareth weaved an excuse.

"Well it's good to see you. Hilda and I visit his grave quite often, making sure it's kept tidy, bring some flowers." As Roy spoke, his wife laid fresh flowers by the headstone, lifting a previous bunch that had begun wilting.

"It must have been awful for you being there when Daniel had the accident," Roy commiserated. "They put you through a most unpleasant time."

Gareth nodded, but wished the man wouldn't start talking about the event.

"Yes, Roy and me thought it was cruel for the police to suspect you of not telling the truth about it," Hilda continued her husband's sentiment. "And when the local paper reported you'd been questioned by the police twice, the rumours building up that there'd been foul play must have been terrible for you."

Gareth nodded again, now distinctly uncomfortable about that past being dredged up.

"You were his best friend," Roy chipped in, "we know you would have done everything in your power to save him."

"Anyway, I suppose none of us want to keep reliving the awful time," said Hilda. "Enough that we no longer have our wonderful son." Her face saddened, growing near to tears.

"Come on ol' girl, we know we'll all be reunited again when our time comes," Roy put a comforting arm round his wife's shoulders.

"Sorry Gareth," Hilda raised a smile for him. "It's just that sometimes…" her words fell away.

Gareth's discomfort now became an urge to get away from the scene as soon as possible, but he had to stay a little longer as the couple stood silently praying for a while.

"Why don't you come back to our place and have a cup of tea," Roy invited when they'd finished.

"Er…" Gareth wrestled, rapidly thinking of a good excuse to decline.

"I've promised to take my daughters to a skating rink later today," a random reply arose. "Need to count in the traffic delays that might build up as I near London."

"You've daughters? We didn't know. You should have told us," said Roy.

"How old are they?" asked Hilda.

"Eight, they're twins," replied Gareth. "Sophie and Amelia."

"How wonderful," the couple expressed their joy learning the news.

"I remember Daniel saying you'd become engaged to a young lady whose name, I'm sorry to say, I've forgotten," said Hilda.

"Melanie," Gareth reminded her. "We're married now."

"Ah yes, Melanie," Hilda remembered.

"You must come and visit us with your wife and children, we'd love to meet them," Roy enthused.

"Yes, we'll have to arrange something," Gareth felt compelled to agree, although he had no intention of ever following through.

"Anyway, I'd better get going. Don't want the girls to miss their ice skating," Gareth was keen to get away before being asked to update contact information. He said farewell and headed for the lych gate exit.

Climbing into his car for the return journey, he felt relieved to get away from the reminder of those hellish times living under suspicion of a crime. As he prepared to start the engine, new company arrived beside him in the shape of Daniel Merriman, making a sudden appearance on the passenger seat. Gareth flinched in shock, his heart racing.

"You didn't even bring me flowers," the unwelcome entity chastised, while his former friend remained speechless, regaining his composure.

"Well you certainly have my parents fooled. They actually believe you're as pure as the driven snow." Daniel shook his head. "They're far too good for the likes of you."

"Why won't you leave me alone," Gareth regained his power of speech. "For years you were gone, until..."

"...that fateful day," Daniel completed. "Why haven't I remained dead, you're wondering."

For a moment there was silence, as the spirit studied Gareth's mournful expression before replying.

"When you were on holiday at Falcombe Sands with your wife and the children," Daniel began, "something began to draw me back. The place where it all began seemed to summon me, as if there was unfinished business. Until then I floated in what felt an endless, timeless void, just existing without form." Daniel paused, looking out the car window across to the church.

"I was never in there, the graveyard," he continued. "Only my body. Not my soul. I suppose I was in some sort of limbo between life and eternal rest, my soul restless because justice for the way I summarily died had not been satisfied."

"I became aware of life again as you walked across the beach with those ice creams," the spirit explained. "Then you fell over catching sight of me. It was at that moment the wrong you'd done to me came streaming back into memory. A wrong carried out by the person I thought my truest friend. The one who I thought would stand by me through thick and thin." Daniel stared accusingly at Gareth. "How stupid I was. Do you really think I would have exposed your illegal sideline?"

"I'm so sorry, I wish I could turn back the clock so that none of it ever happened," Gareth despairingly voiced his regret.

"I bet you do," Daniel's usual laid back delivery had darkened. "From the moment I returned and saw you on the beach, I made it my mission to seek revenge."

Gareth was about to make a plea for clemency, but the ghost disappeared.

****

THE POWERFUL beat vibrating across the venue, pumped high dance energy into the night clubbers, with ever changing colourful swirls of light driving the atmosphere.

Melanie had just finished dancing with Gareth, and they returned to join Daniel chatting with a group of friends at the side of the hall.

"I'm sure your fiancée won't mind me having a dance with you," he said to Melanie, briefly glancing at Gareth to see his reaction. A nod from him granted consent, and they made their way into the rhythmic flow.

"Your future husband is keeping an eagle eye on us," said Daniel. "I think he's worried I'm trying to steal you away." Melanie glanced across and detected Gareth giving a disapproving frown.

When she turned back to Daniel he began to fade away, along with the dancers and music. Only Gareth remained, shaking his head at her.

Melanie woke in bed, staring at the room ceiling, dimly lit by a street light filtering through the curtain. The dream didn't frighten her like last time, when Daniel had turned into a skeleton, but added to the mystery surrounding him since he'd first made that unwelcome intrusion into the house. Why on earth was he, without any reason she could think of, appearing in her dreams?

Remembering now the one when he suddenly turned into a skeleton sent a shiver through her. Was he dead? Was some inexplicable other world message being conveyed in the dream? Melanie's disbelief in all things occult and supernatural dismissed the idea.

The dreams kept playing in her mind. Daniel Merriman dancing with her, and the disapproving look from her husband in the latest one. What was that about? Does Gareth know this person? Is he hiding something from her? Melanie struggled to put some logical explanation together. She couldn't recall ever meeting Merriman in the past, let alone dancing with him.

She remained wide awake, thoughts of her present situation now beginning to surface. The lumpiness of the single bed mattress in her mother's spare room, the awareness of being away from home. The children sharing a double bed in the room beside hers. The sound of her mother's snoring in the room opposite on the landing.

How she longed to be back home with everything as it was before this Merriman person had arrived in their lives. The time when Gareth was a perfectly happy, loving family man, not the angry, morose, troubled character he'd become. How she wished she could penetrate the barrier he'd erected, and perhaps guide him to a solution.

Unable to settle into sleep again she turned on the bedside lamp, illuminating wardrobe, mirrored dresser, chair, olive carpet and curtains, and a couple of floral prints on the wall above the bed. Then she made her way downstairs in her light blue nightdress to make a cup of tea in the kitchen.

CHAPTER 10

ON return from his trip to the churchyard at Cattleford, Gareth heated yet another ready meal in the microwave, then settled again in the living to watch TV with glass of whisky in hand and the bottle beside.

Ways to rid himself of the accursed visitations filled his mind, rather than the antics and sound of some people laughing and cavorting around on the screen in front.

He still retained the local newspaper cuttings reporting the incident at Falcombe Sands all those years ago. At the time he'd meticulously cut out and pasted them into an album, keeping a record of the unfolding investigation into Daniel Merriman's death.

Although he wished at the time it would all go away, there was an urge for him to capture the printed event in the papers. For the first time in his life, the feeling of being someone, a focal point of interest, gave him a strange thrill he'd never experienced before. Fame, no matter how negative, bestowed him with a sense of importance.

As time went by, and he returned into obscurity, the newspaper record became unimportant to him. But he couldn't let go of the documentation, and had retained the album in a securely locked metal storage box in the loft.

Melanie had asked about this secured container, but Gareth had passed it off as having some childhood toys and personal possessions that he liked to keep private.

"You'd only laugh at the silly things," he dismissed her curiosity. She didn't persist, considering it no big deal. And there it rested.

As the TV played on, Gareth began to consider the newspaper reports in the locked box could be the root of his present troubles. It was these remnants of that past stirring them up again he started to convince himself, and not really anything to do with the visit to Falcombe Sands. Time to do something about it he resolved.

He went upstairs to the landing, lowered the loft ladder and climbed in to retrieve the box, taking it back to the living room and entering the opening numbers on the combination lock. Curiosity compelled him to take a look through some of the album cuttings.

One began:

SEA DRAMA PROBE

Police are continuing to question Gareth Richards, the man accompanying Daniel Merriman who was lost overboard on a fishing trip off Falcombe Sands coastline on Wednesday .

Another issue of the paper was headlined:

MISSING MAN'S BODY WASHED ASHORE

The body of a man believed to be Daniel Merriman, lost overboard on a fishing trip off Falcombe Sands, has been found on a beach at Mulligan Cove, three miles down the coast.

A few other issues of the paper contained follow-up stories, including Gareth being released from any further questioning over how Merriman met his fate.

The articles now seemed to be a chain binding him to the past. Time to dispose of them and put the undesirable episode of his life in the bin. Rid himself of Merriman.

Taking the album to the refuse bin at the side of the house, Gareth dumped the previous era of his life into it. Returning indoors, he felt a great sense of relief, freed from the shackles of guilt. Settling on the sofa again, he muted the TV and rang Melanie.

"How are the children?" he asked.

"They seem happy enough," she replied.

"Happy enough? That doesn't exactly sound joyful."

"Well I'm sure they'd prefer to be back home, living the life they did before, as I would too."

"Then come home," Gareth urged, hoping there was a chance of restoring normality. Melanie didn't immediately respond. He sensed her emotions wavering in turmoil.

"I think we need to give it a little longer," she ventured.

"Why? What difference will that make?"

The difference Melanie hoped it would make, lay in her wanting him to appreciate the stability and warmth given by the family life that had once existed for them. That it might stop him obsessing about this Daniel Merriman. Even she had been affected by it with those strange dreams.

After the occasions when the intruder initially entered their lives, getting into the house, the garden and collecting the children from school, as far as she was aware he was no longer on the scene.

Whatever effect he may have had on Gareth's life in the past, now was the time to put the episode behind. But she didn't want to lecture him at that moment and risk another argument.

"I just think it best to give it a bit longer," Melanie concluded.

Gareth didn't want to argue now either. He'd attempt to persuade her another time.

"Can I speak to the children?" he changed focus.

"They're out at the minute, my mother's taken them to a fair at the local recreation ground near here."

It annoyed Gareth that his mother-in-law was enjoying time with Sophie and Amelia, an occasion he should be sharing with them. But he let it pass.

Saying goodbye, he ended the call and reached for the bottle of whisky on the small table nearby to pour another drink. He unmuted the television and started watching a film that was just starting. But the opening scene of a man running down a darkened street pursued by two gunmen hardly registered with him.

The effect of his whisky consumption was now coursing through his body enough to create a relaxing frame of mind. And coupled with the relief of binning past events contained in the newspaper cuttings, he truly believed his troubles were nearly over. He felt confident Melanie would soon relent and come home.

After a couple more glasses, Gareth made his way upstairs to bed on slightly wobbly legs, looking forward to enjoying his first restful sleep since Daniel Merriman had reentered his life.

****

SUNLIGHT flowed brightly through the bedroom window, unimpeded by the curtains Gareth had forgotten to close in his euphoric haze of alcohol. Even with the rough edges of a hangover, his spirits were considerably raised by the newly felt freedom of jettisoning the unfortunate past he'd held in print for so long.

Dragging on his clothing, which laid in a heap by the bedside, he went downstairs to make coffee in the kitchen. As he entered, that new freedom began to evaporate. The album containing the cuttings he'd binned last night rested near the kettle on the counter, seeming to gloat at him.

Had someone seen him disposing of it? Brought it inside to play a trick on him? Had he left a door unlocked, giving them access?

Gareth tried the side door in the utility room leading to the bin beside the house. It was locked. He checked the front door. That was locked. He desperately wanted to find an earthly reason for its return. The alternative explanation would destroy his self awarded exoneration from past events. The torment would go on.

He picked up the album, now intending to burn it in the garden. A voice came from behind. Gareth turned to see Daniel Merriman standing in the kitchen doorway.

"You never had the guts to confess the truth to the police back then, so you can serve your sentence now," pronounced the spirit, and disappeared.

Gareth grasped his head in both hands, shaking it in despair. He was in a fortress prison guarded by the most impenetrable walls and security. A ghost.

Unable to face going into work, he rang to say he had a heavy cold, which would have been highly preferable to the tortuous ill he was truly suffering.

After making a coffee, he called Melanie. His mother-in-law answered.

"Where's Melanie?" he asked tersely, not wishing to converse with the woman he disliked intensely.

"She's gone to the shops and left her phone behind," Evelyn replied. "What do you want?" She had the same desire not to speak with her unworthy son-in-law.

"Nothing. I'll call later." Gareth hung up. He felt the need to get some fresh air to clear his thoughts, and decided to go for a walk.

The urban setting of the house didn't offer much in the way of refreshing air, with cars, trucks and buses frequently passing on the road, but those were largely a distant event as he strolled along the pavement concentrating on his present dilemma. He'd disposed of Merriman in life, but now he needed to dispose of him in death. A trickier task, to say the least, than on the first occasion.

As he continued his walk, he saw the Lord Raglan pub a short distance ahead. He was a fairly frequent visitor to the place on a Sunday lunchtime, though hadn't been in for his couple of beers there since the Merriman business had kicked off.

The premises dated back to the 19th century with original oak ceiling beams still visible. But subsequent chain restaurant groups had added tacky makeovers and additions, so that plastic upholstery and fake beams in the extensions had helped to destroy any old world ambience.

Gareth, however, like many of its customers, was more concerned with the availability of getting a drink, and occasionally eating a passable mostly microwaved meal with his family. On this visit alcohol was his main driver.

"Hello Gareth, haven't seen you here for a while. The usual?" Phil, the manager, greeted him with a smile rising on his crinkly face. Gareth nodded.

Wearing a white shirt with patterned red tie and black trousers, the middle-aged man had a few wisps of remaining silvery hair brushed neatly back on his head, and carried a portly stomach from years of generously tasting his pub's ales.

A man and woman with drinks chatted nearby at the bar. A few tables were occupied in the large saloon, but there wasn't much trade this early in the day.

"I'll be leaving here soon," Phil imparted, after dispensing the beer and placing it on the counter, while Gareth tapped his card on the payment register.

"Head office is getting a new manager to run the place," Phil continued. "Lovely lady, but doesn't have a lot of experience in the pub trade. Wish her well though, everyone has to start somewhere."

He paused thoughtfully for a moment. "These aren't really pubs anymore though, are they? All turning into restaurants. People like me with years of experience in the trade, all being turned out to graze." Phil looked gloomy for a moment, but quickly recovered his customer friendly persona developed over many years.

While he chatted on, Gareth stood at the bar with the man's opinions and tales of current events drifting along elsewhere.

"Oh, I nearly forgot. Someone came in here yesterday looking for you," the publican's change of conversation brought Gareth back to his surroundings.

"Who?" he now gave his full attention.

"I don't know. He didn't leave his name," replied Phil. "It wasn't a local customer."

"What did he look like?"

"I don't know. My wife Peggy was bar serving at the time. I wasn't here." Phil was surprised at Gareth's terse questioning, unaware of his present stress level.

"Peggy wrote down his number on a piece of paper. It's over here." Phil turned and took it from the counter beneath the optics. Gareth dialled the number.

"Hello," came a man's voice. "Cartwright Funeral Services. How may I help you?"

Gareth didn't answer, his face growing ashen. The man repeated his question. Gareth hung up.

"Are you alright?" The barman noticed the drawn expression and blanched face of his customer, now turning to head for the exit.

"You haven't finished your beer," Phil called.

Gareth had no intention of explaining to the publican that the number he'd called was the company who'd arranged Daniel Merriman's funeral.

****

DANIEL and Gareth sat opposite each other at the Indian restaurant enjoying a curry, a bottle of white wine in an ice bucket on the table, and two glasses close to nearing refills.

"We've been working together at Shaw's accountancy firm for five years now, and I've been wondering if we should venture out and start our own firm as partners," Daniel suggested, after finishing a mouthful of chicken biryani.

"I'm not sure," said Gareth, taking a sip of wine. "It's a bit risky."

"Oh come on, we need to break out," insisted Daniel, "establish a business that sees we make good money for ourselves, for our future, instead of Shaw's directors making a mint through our hard work."

"I take your point, but I'm getting married to Melanie soon, and I want the security of setting up home, and maybe us having children in the near future with a regular income. It isn't a good time for me to start taking a risk that could jeopardise it," Gareth was not convinced of branching out just yet.

"We've got good contacts, we could probably convince them to change from Shaw's to us," Daniel persisted.

"We've signed contracts saying we won't poach clients from Shaw's for year after leaving their employment," Gareth pointed out.

"We'll find other clients in the meantime," Daniel reached for the wine bottle, topping up his colleague's glass. Gareth remained unconvinced.

"Anyway, think about it." Daniel took another mouthful of food, and they were silent for a while.

"I'm throwing a birthday party in a couple of weeks, and would love you and Melanie to come," Daniel changed subject.

"That we can agree on," Gareth lifted a forkful of rice to his mouth.

****

MELANIE and Gareth stood outside the ground floor door of the apartment building where Daniel lived, waiting for him to answer the bell.

She wore a short, black denim skirt and white blouse, with Gareth dressed in a red polo shirt and blue cargo trousers.

"Lovely to see you both," Daniel greeted them as they entered, handing him a wrapped birthday present. Music pounded from the living room, where friends danced as their host, in an open neck teal shirt and buff chinos, led them inside.

A woman with cropped fair hair, dancing with a man, looked across at them raising her hand in greeting. She wore a knee length yellow dress, covered with stars and crescents glitter reflecting brightly in the light.

"Who's that?" asked Gareth, not recognizing her.

"Dilys. Dilys Foster. We met a few weeks ago. She owns Twingles, the clothes shop on the high street near our office."

"Getting serious with her?" Gareth probed.

"Don't be so nosy," Melanie slapped his wrist.

"No," Daniel laughed. "We've been out a few times, but more just friends at the minute." He glanced at Melanie. "Now while Dilys is dancing with someone else, may I have the pleasure of dancing with you?"

She smiled and chatted with him as they weaved across the floor between other smiling couples. Gareth felt yet another surge of jealousy. Melanie seemed to be getting too familiar with his friend on these social occasions.

A woman nearby, holding a glass of wine at the side of the room, approached to talk with him, but he ignored her. Gareth was immersed in noting every sign of enjoyment his fiancée seemed to be having with his work colleague, who until recently, he thought a trusted friend. When the music paused for a moment, Melanie returned to Gareth.

"You seemed to be having a great time dancing with Daniel," he glowered.

"Yes, he's great fun," Melanie laughed, now in the party spirit. "He's certainly enjoying his birthday."

"What were you talking about?" Gareth demanded.

"He was just saying you are a lucky man having someone as beautiful as me as his fiancée," Melanie laughed again.

"Did he?" Gareth glanced across at the other side of the room seeing Daniel and Dilys chatting with friends. The partygoers began dancing to a new song striking up.

"It looked like he was trying to get close to you, reaching out to put his arms round you," Gareth accused.

"He's probably had a bit too much to drink. Just a bit of harmless fun," Melanie's rising party spirit was beginning to slip away, realising her fiancée suspected Daniel of trying to steal her from him.

"I think you're being ridiculous," Melanie grew serious. "Daniel said if I had been engaged to anyone else but you, he would have moved heaven and earth to try and make me his own. But you are his greatest friend, and that he wished us all the happiness in the world in our married life together."

Gareth woke in bed, cold sweat streaming from him.

CHAPTER 11

THE morning was grey, steeped in a cloud layer threatening a downpour at any time, as Gareth sipped his coffee in the kitchen

The gloomy light coming through the window matched his mood. After that dream had resurfaced of a past event in his life at Daniel's party, he couldn't settle into a restful sleep. He had to do something to make the continued visitations and apparent punishments being delivered by his deceased former friend go away.

Perhaps confession would be the only route of escape, though there would be unpleasant consequences. But at least those would be earthbound, and not coming from a source beyond human control, which might last to the end of his days. Or even shorten them through stressful illness.

He considered the option within his control, while making another coffee and resisting the strong urge to bury his dilemma in alcohol.

Entering the hall to check a pad on the telephone table listing useful numbers, he lifted the landline phone beside it and dialled the local police.

"I want to make a confession," he said to the woman answering his call.

"Hold on," she replied, "I'm putting you through to another section."

Gareth lost his nerve and hung up. He wandered with his coffee into the garden, feeling a light drizzle in the air. The thought of serving time behind bars terrified him as the reality vividly dawned. He'd be separated from his family for

God knows how many years. At least on the outside he could redeem himself with Melanie. But Merriman, how to deal with him, a spirit?

The drizzle began to give way to rain, rapidly increasing intensity. Gareth returned inside. The urge to move from coffee to whisky grew stronger. He continued to resist, wanting to think of a credible way out of his troubles without alcohol clouding his mind.

He entered the living room, once a relaxing haven. Perhaps if he made himself comfortable and pushed stress aside, a clearer picture of the way forward would emerge. He was about to settle on the sofa, when the doorbell rang.

Gareth's heart leapt with uncontrollable hope that it could be Melanie returning with the children. But she had a key. Hope began to fade. Why would she ring the doorbell? And surely she would have phoned to say she was coming home first?

He opened the door to see two uniformed policemen.

"Hello sir," spoke one, sergeant rank stripes displayed on the arms of his coat. "We've received a call from your phone linked to this address. Is that correct?" The officer stared inquisitively from his work weary middle years face for an answer. A much younger constable beside him had softer features, not yet shaped by dramas of the job.

Gareth hadn't realised that his number would be traced. He was tempted to deny he'd rung, but that would cause suspicion and might make matters worse.

"Yes, it was me."

"Is there a problem? We understand you were calling to make some confession," the sergeant probed.

Gareth faltered, desperately trying to downplay his call. "I was being a bit silly. Something I'd done a long time ago has been troubling me. It's nothing earth shattering. Just something I did that's been preying on my mind."

Both officers gave him a puzzled look, not entirely convinced Gareth was hiding something trivial.

"May we come in sir?" asked the sergeant, more by way of command than request. Both of them also had the pressing desire to get out of the increasing downpour.

Gareth stood aside as they entered and led them into the kitchen, where the officers identified themselves.

"I'm Sergeant Derek Holland and this is Constable Mark Dreyfus. Now what is this confession you want to make?" The sergeant's tone was becoming abrasive. He didn't like Gareth's evasive shifty eyes that seemed to indicate he was preparing to tell a lie. The younger constable didn't need years of experience to conclude this too.

"Well, some years ago I stole a coat from a shop," Gareth said, unable to face revealing his true crime.

"How many years ago did you steal this coat?" the sergeant asked.

"It was a long time ago," Gareth began shuffling uneasily.

"Which shop?" the younger officer picked up his superior's thread.

"It was years ago. I can't remember its name."

The target of the officers' questions grew more uncomfortable, intertwining his fingers in agitation.

"Can you remember where this shop is?" the constable threw in another question, while Sergeant Holland looked on analytically.

"In…" Gareth hesitated, attempting to think of some location. If only he'd been prepared for this visit.

"Well, it would be difficult for us to check the records for a report about a stolen coat from a shop you can't remember, in a place you can't recall, or the year it happened." The sergeant came in again with growing impatience.

"Do you still have this coat?" he followed rapidly with another question.

"Er, no," Gareth could now feel sweat leaking from his forehead.

"Is there anything else you'd like to ask this gentleman?" the sergeant turned to his colleague, putting contemptuous emphasis on the word 'gentleman'.

"No sir," he replied.

"Right," the lead officer stared grimly at Gareth. "I could arrest you for wasting police time," he warned, leaving the threat hanging for a few moments to let Gareth sweat further. "If you do that again, I will have no hesitation in arresting you and charging you with the offence. I will also make sure any other officer called out by you on a false claim is aware of the situation."

To make sure Gareth got the message, the younger officer joined his sergeant with a disapproving look, then both turned and left the house.

Gareth was about to make his way to the living room and pour a whisky to steady his nerves, when Daniel Merriman appeared in front of him.

"That went well," the spirit laughed, and disappeared.

****

NEXT morning Gareth decided to go into work. As he gazed at himself in the bathroom mirror it shocked him to see the drawn dark shadows under his eyes. The stress and excessive drink was taking its toll. Smartening himself and dressing in his charcoal suit, he left for work.

Entering the building, colleagues passing through reception enquired if he was feeling better. He nodded while making his way to the lift.

In his office he checked the numerous emails that had accumulated in his absence, answering the most pressing. The desk phone rang.

"Gareth," came the man's voice, "glad you're back. Feeling better now?"

Gareth confirmed that he was, but wondered why his boss, Gerald Hodges, was calling.

"Pop in and see me for a minute. I'd like to have a chat," Hodges instructed.

Gareth replaced the phone. Had the police been in touch to tell his boss about their visit? Why would they do that? He'd been given a warning. Surely that was the end of the matter? He made his way along the corridor to the office marked Gerald Hodges, Accounts Director, in gold lettering on the door.

"Come in, come in," the man invited, as Gareth knocked. He entered, seeing a broadly built man in a dark grey suit sitting behind a richly polished mahogany desk.

"Take a seat," the director indicated the brown leather upholstered chair facing his desk, a faint smile on his tanned face from a recent holiday abroad. He brushed back his dyed brown hair hiding the grey clue of middle age, then straightened his blue tie, bearing the insignia of a gold golf ball, indicating his exclusive membership of a golfing club.

"Something seems to be distracting you in your work," Gareth's superior began, switching eye focus between employee and computer screen on his desk. Gareth was about to respond, but Hodges continued.

"It shows here that some of your reports have not been fully completed. Work that should have been completed even before you were off work for a while." The boss waited for a reply.

"I'm sorry, I wasn't aware of that," Gareth replied.

"No, obviously not," agreed Hodges. "And I've heard from your colleagues that your mind seems to be elsewhere these days, distracted. Would that be fair comment?"

"Well I suppose I've had a lot on my mind recently…domestic stuff," Gareth offered a reason.

"I'm sorry to hear that. We all go through a rough patch on the home front from time to time I suppose," his director empathised. "But we can't let it disrupt our business. Small mistakes can cost us a lot of money, as I'm sure you appreciate."

Gareth could only agree, offering apology again.

"I suggest you take a couple of weeks off on full pay. Work out your problems, and come back refreshed," Hodges advised.

"I'm sure I can carry on working. I'll pay more attention in future," Gareth insisted.

His boss leaned back in his chair, considering his next words.

"You are a valued senior member of this organisation, Gareth. I would hate to be in the position of taking further steps that would be detrimental to your career here, due to the recent lower standard of work." The director delivered his veiled threat. "Please take my advice seriously." Hodges gazed with searching eyes, hoping his employee would accept the offer.

"If you think that would be the best course, then yes I'll take the time off," Gareth conceded, not wishing to take the path towards possible demotion or unemployment.

"Very wise," the boss delivered in a solemn tone.

****

AT HOME that evening, Gareth sat on the sofa in the living room and rang his wife. If he was to restore some part of his broken life, the first part would be having his family back with him.

"Hello daddy," Amelia greeted him.

"Hello darling," Gareth was thrilled to hear his daughter's voice, "how are you my lovely?"

"Grandma gave us cakes and hot chocolate with marshmallows this afternoon," she told him excitedly.

"That sounds wonderful," her father enthused, though inwardly annoyed by any activity Evelyn did to ingratiate herself with his daughters.

"Tomorrow she's promised to take us to the zoo," delight for the forthcoming trip bubbled in the youngster.

"Has she?" was the only response Gareth could summon. "Is mummy there?"

For a moment he heard background sounds of voices, then Melanie came on.

"I think Amelia has been keeping you up to speed on what they've been doing, and their trip tomorrow," she laughed. "She knows how to use this phone better than me. Always catching her playing games on it."

Gareth was delighted to hear his wife's lighthearted mood, and felt it a good moment to make his plea for her to return home. He delivered his pitch. There was silence for a moment.

"Look, I really don't want to go through all that right now," her mood became downbeat.

"I really do miss you all," Gareth persisted. Another silence came.

"Can we discuss this another time?"

"Okay, but please think about it," Gareth pleaded.

"I will," Melanie promised, "and before you go, Sophie wants a word."

Gareth spoke to his other daughter, generally getting a repeat of Amelia's conversation, but with more detail about the cakes they'd eaten. When the call ended, he settled back in the sofa and turned on the television.

At first his thoughts remained on the conversation he'd had with his wife, wondering in the tone of her reply if there was a hint of her wanting to return home. She hadn't turned down his request outright. There was hope he decided.

Gradually his mind began to be drawn by the quiz on the TV, and he found himself attempting to answer the questions.

In a split second the programme disappeared to be replaced by Daniel Merriman's grinning face. Gareth grabbed the remote to turn off the TV, but it didn't respond. Next moment the quiz show was restored to the screen, as the ghost materialised on the sofa beside Gareth.

"It's been a long time since I've watched TV. How are you getting along answering the quiz questions?" the uninvited guest asked.

Gareth was unable to speak at first, coming to terms with the sudden appearance beside him of his ghostly nemesis.

"Coming back from the dead has been a bit of a quiz for me too," Daniel continued, without waiting for his former friend to reply to his question.

"Technology has been racing along for the past decade, since last I was here alive. So many gadgets and streamlining. And so much more has happened in the world. I've been catching up all over the place. It's useful being a ghost with no barriers to stop you going anywhere," Daniel paused, glancing at Gareth. "On the other hand, I'd give a lot to have a drink of your whisky or a beer, eat a good meal. That's the downside of being a spirit, unable to enjoy things like I once did."

"What can I do to stop you haunting me?" Gareth pleaded desperately, regaining his power of speech. "I'm at my wits end. You're destroying my life."

"Well you certainly destroyed mine," Daniel sneered. "What do you reckon you could do to restore that, old friend?" he highlighted the impasse between them.

"The blue whale," called Daniel, his attention drawn to the television, leaving Gareth entirely confused.

"The quiz Gareth, weren't you paying attention? The question was what is the largest animal in the world. The blue whale. See, I'm right, the correct answer is now displaying in green," Daniel pointed at the screen.

The change in conversation from serious to trivia annoyed Gareth, but he didn't react. The spirit continued giving answers to the quiz questions. Then the screen went blank.

"It's okay, there's nothing wrong with the set," Daniel reassured. "When you're a ghost you can turn TVs on and off at will." The spirit gazed at Gareth, noting the drawn expression around his eyes, brought on by the stress. "To think once we were the greatest of friends. But now, once again, you'd do anything to be rid of me," he shook his head in disappointment.

"Well, I have a solution for you. If you do as I ask, I will leave you in peace, and it will allow me to reach my next destiny," the spirit offered.

Gareth turned his head to gaze back at Daniel, hope in the eyes of hopelessness beginning to dawn.

"What would you like me to do?" his former companion asked eagerly, though wary of what he wanted.

"I want you to hire a boat in a month's time on the 25th, and go out to the spot where we last went sea fishing off the coast of Falcombe Sands."

"Is that all?" It didn't sound a difficult proposal. Gareth had expected more of a request.

"That is all," Daniel confirmed. " I would just like us to return to the area where we once had enjoyable times fishing together. I'll join you for a while, then I'll leave you alone. Better that we part this way, than last time." He smiled at his erstwhile companion.

"And you're sure that is all?" Gareth still found it hard to believe it would be so simple to stop the hauntings.

"That is all," Daniel repeated. "Why, don't you trust me?"

"It's just that I thought I'd have to do more to redeem myself."

"That's your guilt plaguing you, not me."

"Yes, I suppose so."

"Before I leave for now, I want you to explain something," said Daniel, with a puzzled frown.

"If I can," Gareth replied.

"I've been following your life since I returned, as you probably know, but I'm puzzled about a particular thing."

"What's that?"

"Your wife Melanie seems to have no recollection of me. She knew me well when years back you and I worked together. How can she have forgotten me?"

"That's easy to explain," Gareth relaxed at the thought that he could soon be rid of this spirit.

"Do you mind if I have a drink?" he asked, yearning for some strong liquid refreshment.

"Not at all, only wish I could join you. Having no proper body makes it difficult. But you go ahead," Daniel waved his ethereal arm in consent, prompting Gareth to cross to the drinks cabinet and pour a generous glass of whisky. He returned to sit on the side facing armchair beside the sofa, feeling more comfortable resting there than beside the ghost.

"She fell down a long flight of steps in an office building where she'd worked. It was about a year after we got married," Gareth explained, shaking his head recalling the event. "Such a worrying time. She was in a coma for a few days with a head injury. Thankfully she came round, but it left her with some memory loss. There are periods of her life she just can't recall."

"Ah, I understand," said Daniel, taking in the revelation. "So Melanie doesn't remember me when I was alive, or when I died."

"No, like us, she lived a long way from the area. She'd only been to Falcombe Bay before when she was young," Gareth continued to explain. "I wasn't married to her when you and me went on our last..." he hesitated as guilt again surfaced, "...fishing trip. Melanie just thought we'd extended it. The news about your death was mostly in the local media, and she didn't see any coverage"

"So there wasn't any time before her fall when she asked about me? Where I was?" Daniel sounded a little hurt.

90

"She did ask, but I told her you'd set up your own business in another part of the country. Of course they obviously knew about it at work, and there were some there who suspected I'd had some part in your death. But most took the view it was an accident. Your funeral was held where you'd originally lived, so there was no news or talk about it nearer home."

"And Melanie didn't hear it from anyone else at parties or get togethers from our company afterwards?" the ghost remained puzzled.

"I turned down invites, so she didn't get the chance to hear from others, and you were the only one she had really known from our company," Gareth enlightened him. "I changed jobs soon after, so we no longer mixed with the old crowd anyway."

Daniel absorbed the information, slowly nodding his head.

"But what if she came across some old news stories about the incident? Saw your name and asked who I was?" Daniel posed what would be a tricky situation. "Those cuttings you'd hidden and tried to get rid of?" The question also confirmed that it was him who'd returned them overnight from the bin to the house.

The possibility of Melanie hearing about the incident was something Gareth had considered.

"Obviously I'd have to tell her it happened, but as the cuttings also show, I was later exonerated. I'd say I hadn't told her because it would have upset her."

"You always were a bit of a devious sod," Daniel commented. Gareth didn't reply, taking another drink of whisky.

"So, as we agreed," the ghost rose from the sofa. "In a month's time, hire the boat for the 25th and go to the area off the coast where we last fished."

Gareth confirmed agreement to the deal.

"Now you can work on restoring your life with Melanie and the children," Daniel advised, then disappeared. In the same moment the TV came on again.

Gareth relaxed back on the sofa, looking forward to achieving normality in his life again. And then it came to him. The 25th would be exactly ten years since Daniel departed this life.

CHAPTER 12

EVELYN entered the spare bedroom upstairs where Melanie sat at a table compiling an office report on the laptop.

"Would you like a cup of tea dear?" she asked her daughter.

"Yes please mum," Melanie replied, continuing to work.

Before leaving the room, Evelyn crossed to the window overlooking the neatly trimmed front garden lawn with a circular central flower bed.

"Oh," she uttered.

"What's the matter?" her daughter kept concentrating on the work. Evelyn frequently paid visits to what Melanie considered her inner sanctum while she was working, and found it increasingly annoying.

"Just a matter of your husband coming down the garden path," her mother announced frostily.

"What!" Melanie's attention rapidly switched away from work and she crossed to the window.

"Well I haven't invited him here," she said, sensing Evelyn's suspicion of an arrangement behind her back.

"I hope it doesn't end up with me having to call the police," mother's frostiness had turned into a block of ice.

"You're taking it to extremes," Melanie was preparing to defuse escalation of full scale war developing between both parties. She was also wary of Gareth's uninvited visit. The doorbell rang. She went downstairs to answer the call.

He stood there, dressed in a black suede jacket, light blue open neck shirt, charcoal pleated trousers and black shoes. Melanie hadn't seen this outfit before, and it looked as though her husband had made a special effort to present himself in a new light. She noted his right arm was behind his back, and in a sweeping move he brought it forward presenting a bunch of red roses.

"I've come to apologise for behaving so badly, and promise to be on my best behaviour in future," he pledged, handing her the flowers.

Melanie wasn't convinced that he could keep such a promise, but his gesture softened her feelings towards him. She didn't enjoy their separation, and although she loved her mother, living with Evelyn as an adult was a very different experience to the days when she was younger.

Her mother meant well, but couldn't get used to the idea her daughter didn't need the shepherding that formed mother's role in past years.

"Ah Evelyn," Gareth saw the woman standing behind his wife delivering him a glowering cold stare. "I apologise to you too."

"Has he been drinking again?" she whispered to her daughter, unmoved by her son-in-law's apology. Melanie ignored her.

"Can I come in?" asked Gareth.

"Tell him to go away," Evelyn directed.

"Be quiet mum," Melanie was growing annoyed by the prompting. She accepted it was her mother's house, but didn't think it would hurt for him to enter for a moment. She stood aside to let him in.

"I don't want any trouble," she demanded. "We can go into the living room, you can have your say, then I'll decide. Though I can guess what you want."

Gareth smiled at her and complied, entering the room that he'd been in before, but had made a point not to visit regularly since it required meeting her disapproving mother.

Evelyn joined them, after being handed the flowers by her daughter to put on the kitchen counter. She stood sternly in the doorway observing them, as Melanie invited Gareth to sit in an armchair. At this stage she didn't wish him to be beside her on the sofa.

"Yes, you know why I've come," he said. "Truly I have changed, realising just how much you mean to me," Gareth pleaded his case. "Things just got on top of me, which I found hard to control. But now they're all sorted." His plaintiff, almost tearful face softened her feelings further. "I miss you and the children. We can be happy again."

Evelyn desperately wanted to pour scorn on his pleading, though resisted, even enjoying her least favourite person begging forgiveness.

"And Evelyn, I want to apologise to you too," Gareth directed his gaze at her. "I've been unjustifiably offhand with you, and it has caused me deep regret."

The woman's steely barrier, always erected in the presence of her son-in-law, wobbled for a moment, unprepared for this unexpected peace offering. She didn't know how to respond. Was it genuine, or an act to win her over for his own devious purpose? Her wavering soon resolved itself.

She opted for him plotting some underhand ploy, and her barrier firmly re-established itself.

Deciding any advice warning her daughter to treat Gareth's promises with caution would be dismissed, Evelyn left for the kitchen to make herself a cup of tea.

"I don't think I could ever say anything to make your mother think better of me," Gareth said.

"She has a cynical attitude about many things in life," Melanie reflected, after closing the living room door to lessen further access of Evelyn's prying ears. "My mother used to be very lively and positive until the day my father left her for another woman," her eyes saddened.

Melanie had told Gareth about the event years back in the early days of their marriage, but he'd always assumed her husband had left because she was such a misery. Now he realised it was the cause.

"I'm sorry, I've been a bit of a pigheaded fool," he confessed.

"You have," Melanie wasn't going to let him off the hook lightly.

Gareth wished he could tell her why he'd been behaving so badly and drinking heavily. But, as he'd previously concluded, all his pleas for her and the children to return home would be completely blown apart if he explained the ghost of Daniel was relentlessly pursuing him for a dreadful crime he'd committed years back at Falcombe Sands.

Melanie now returned to the sofa and invited her husband to sit beside her.

"If I agree to come home with the children, how can I be sure you won't start making life difficult again for us all?" she posed the crucial question.

"I can only give you my absolute promise that I will not behave badly again. I've worked through my problems, and I pledge that I will stop drinking alcohol," Gareth sounded convincingly earnest. "You and the children are the most important of all in my life."

Inwardly he prayed he'd made his case. Words were the only assurances he could offer right now, until Melanie and the youngsters returned home where he could demonstrate his promises in action.

His wife didn't relish him begging like this. She wanted him to show penitence, which he did. That was her only desire.

"Well, I'll think it over," she replied, after letting the matter hang for a moment. "Let's speak again tomorrow." Gareth nodded, feeling confident that he had made headway towards restoring a vital part of life again.

"Are the children here?" he asked.

"No, a friend of mine has taken them to a local playgroup," Melanie explained, glancing at her watch. "They'll be there for a couple more hours. It's an outing for them before they go back to school next week from their half term holiday."

Gareth contained his disappointment and felt he'd be overstaying his welcome by asking if he could wait. His wife might consent, but Evelyn would probably hover casting thunderous atmosphere all around. Progress to get on her right side, as Melanie would like, could take a fair bit longer.

"I'd better push on then," he rose from the sofa.

"And I'd better get on with my work before the children come back," Melanie stood up.

"Give my love to Sophie and Amelia," said Gareth at the front door as he was leaving.

"I will."

"And please come home soon," he made another plea just as she began closing the door.

"I'm thinking about it," she offered a crumb of comfort.

Evelyn appeared in the hall from the kitchen when Gareth left. She'd been eavesdropping on their conversation through the living room door.

"I suppose he's wrapping you round his little finger," she delivered cynically. Melanie stood firmly, giving the woman a resolute stare.

"Mum, I appreciate you taking me and the children in during a difficult time, but Gareth is my husband and it would be best if we could live together with the children, who love him very much. And so do I." Melanie laid out her cards.

"Well if you go back, I hope it all works out for you. But don't say I haven't warned you," Evelyn shrugged, turned and walked away.

****

IT took Daniel a while getting used to being a ghost, ever since he'd been invoked into awareness of existence again at Falcombe Sands.

Perhaps Gareth returning on holiday with his family had triggered him back through some inexplicable link between life and death. Being a ghost didn't seem to bestow any greater knowledge about the mysteries of creation beyond his experience of being alive.

Unless possibly remaining in a limbo land because of unfinished business in life, had prevented him from attaining any higher form of knowledge.

There were advantages in not having a tangible form. Passing through barriers was no problem. Moving from one location to another in an instant was an asset that any living person could only envy. And yet, how he yearned to have a real living existence again. Was it possible? He'd been giving that a great deal of thought.

Another inexplicable thing about being a ghost was the ability to feel emotion without any of the physical requirements needed as a human. He regretted visiting Melanie in her home that time not long after he'd awoken as a spirit. He hadn't meant her to fear an intruder had broken in, causing her to worry of possible harm to the children.

He didn't know at the time she suffered from partial memory loss. Though thinking about it, if she had remembered him and he declared he was a ghost, that would likely have terrified her.

It's just that he had grown strongly attracted to her during the time she'd first become Gareth's girlfriend and then fiancée.

But he would never attempt to steal her from him. They were bonded friends, and he could not live easily again if he'd succeeded in doing so. The irony, thought Daniel, was Gareth had carried out an act of treachery on him. Now that had been unnecessary. Uncalled for. The wrong needed putting right.

CHAPTER 13

GARETH opened the front door to be greeted by his daughters throwing their arms around his waist.

"Daddy, it's lovely to be back," they cried. Gareth tousled their hair, glancing at Melanie behind them and giving her a smile.

"It's wonderful to have you home," he told the girls, as they released his waist and dived inside heading to their rooms.

"I've got a treat for you," their father called to them as they ran up the stairs, "come and see me in a minute."

"Welcome home," he greeted Melanie with a kiss on the cheek. "It's wonderful to have you back where you belong." He took the suitcase Melanie was holding, as she stepped inside, and placed it in the hall.

A week after his visit to Evelyn's house, Melanie had agreed to return on a trial basis. Her husband's pledge to stop drinking did allow for an occasional glass of wine or beer.

"That bunch of flowers you had delivered to my mother was probably a bit over the top," Melanie laughed as they entered the kitchen. "But I think it did actually cause a bit of a thaw in the ice she's coated over you."

"I don't think she'll ever like me," Gareth grinned while making coffee, "though it would be good if I could get on a little better at least with her, for all our sakes."

"Well you'll just have to bite your tongue when she says something you disagree with," Melanie laughed again. She felt lifted and happy to be on home territory after the separation, hoping and praying her husband would remain true to his promise of reformation. He already looked healthier and less stressed than she'd seen for some time.

"Where's our treat daddy?" the girls called, descending the stairs after checking their rooms remained as they'd left them, minus some possessions still in the suitcase.

Gareth was handing his wife a mug of coffee as they were preparing to enter the living room, but seeing the children's expectation and joy at being home, the move was temporarily delayed. He opened a kitchen cupboard and took out two cartons of chocolate he knew were their favourite. With eager smiles they quickly began to tear open the packaging.

"You're not to eat them all at once," their mother ordered, as the youngsters began leaving for their rooms.

"No mummy," Amelia declared for herself and sister.

"If you don't eat all your dinner later, I'll know you've disobeyed me."

"Yes mummy," replied Sophie in a resigned tone as they left.

"I expect they'll be frightened to eat the chocolate now," Gareth grinned.

"I doubt it," Melanie knew her orders had limits, although she anticipated they would leave some to eat later. The fact they were happy to be home called for a bit of lee-way.

"Come on then, let's settle with our coffee in the living room together for a while, like we used to," Gareth began to lead the way.

"And I've another treat in store," he said as they settled on the sofa. "I'm taking us all out this evening to that expensive restaurant, as you like to call it."

****

GARETH had extended the restaurant invitation to include his mother-in-law, and to his surprise she'd accepted.

As they ate, Daniel stood invisibly nearby watching the proceedings closely.

"It's all overpriced in these places," Evelyn commented, as she forked a piece of trout to her mouth.

"Stop complaining," Melanie beside her urged. "This is Gareth's treat."

Her mother didn't want to display any sign she was grateful for her son-in-law's invitation to the top rated restaurant, or let him think he'd scored a point over her. She ignored her daughter's plea, continuing to maintain a dour face while eating. Though she was beginning to wonder if Gareth had seen the error of his ways. Time would tell.

The family gathering pleased Daniel, continuing to watch the family unseen.

If Evelyn was avoiding showing any pleasure at the outing, the children didn't hide their enjoyment.

"Can we have ice cream or brownies in a minute?" Sophie asked, still working her way through her main course of vegetarian fajitas.

"I'd like chocolate cake," Amelia felt compelled to add her preference.

"Just finish your meals, or you'll get nothing more," Melanie warned them, indicating with a smile across the table to Gareth that it was just an idle threat.

An unobserved smile also rose on Daniel's face. Harmony in the family was a vital part of his plan.

****

A WARM greeting met Gareth as he entered the office of his boss, Gerald Hodges, seated at his desk. The man beckoned him to sit on the chair opposite.

"So glad to see you back with us, and looking so much better than the last time we had a chat," he said.

Gareth nodded agreement with his superior's comment, though disliked the disingenuous nature of his underlying nature. He was well aware Hodges would step on anyone who defied his orders, or attempted to outshine his position. Past victims proved that.

"I take it the time off I granted you has allowed you to sort out your problems?" the director elevated his act of generosity.

"Thank you for allowing me the time off, yes I'm more settled now." Gareth replied meekly, hoping the director would acknowledge his humble gratitude with kindness. He feared his boss would consider him for lesser duties in a demotion, on the basis he couldn't take the stress of his present position.

"As you know, I highly value the work you do for this organisation and until your recent lapse in health, I had planned to promote you to a divisional manager role."

Hodges' wavered on an uncertain future for Gareth, who had been totally unaware of this plan.

"I am very much better than I was," he insisted, "my health is fully recovered." His fear of going no further in the company seemed to be looming.

"Yes, I realise you're much better than when I last saw you," Hodges continued, resting back in his chair. "And I hope to go ahead with a promotion for you."

The unexpected announcement was no less than a complete shock for Gareth.

"Lance Everton, who holds the divisional manager role for Hindle area at present, is retiring in a month's time," the director explained," and if you maintain your health and show no signs of relapse, I'll be confident in selecting you as his successor."

"Thank you sir. You won't regret it," Gareth promised earnestly. Elevation to a divisional manger job carried a much higher salary, and it would be just the positive change he needed.

Hodges waved his hand, dismissing the presence of his lower ranking employee.

"You won't regret it sir," Gareth repeated his assurance as he left.

Daniel had stood unseen in the office, observing the meeting. Events were progressing in the right direction.

CHAPTER 14

GARETH'S happiness with life, and the restoration of his relationship with Melanie, made it hard for him to tell her a lie. That is, not lying beyond fulfilling the promise he'd made to his former now departed friend. He could hardly tell her that he was going to meet Daniel's spirit offshore at Falcombe Sands.

"It's a day's work conference at a venue in Colchester," he told her one evening as they settled to watch TV after the girls had gone to bed.

"I'll be setting off early to avoid the traffic, but hopefully be back before it's late," Gareth continued the deception.

Melanie nestled her head on his shoulder as the TV came on. Her husband and the children were fundamental to her life, and seeing the family happily reunited again formed the foundation to all else. And, of course, the prospect of Gareth's promotion could only help improve their prospects.

She was unaware of her husband's trepidation at the forthcoming meeting with Daniel. The thoughts going through his mind. Did the spirit genuinely mean to keep his word about never haunting him again if he fulfilled the promise of their reunion at sea? Doubt had begun to surface. But if he decided not to go, what would follow? No, he had to fulfil the agreement.

"Are you alright?" Melanie detected a tenseness in him as she continued to rest her head on his shoulder.

"I'm absolutely fine," he assured her.

****

EARLY morning sunlight grew increasingly brighter through the kitchen window, as Gareth sat at the table eating a bowl of cereal and drinking coffee.

His offshore meeting with Daniel dawned, and he was preparing to leave while Melanie and the children still slept.

He continued to feel nervous anticipation of the event, but at least after today he'd be able to put all the business of Daniel's persecution and general disruption of his life behind him.

It was a three hour drive to Falcombe Sands and he'd arranged to hire a motorboat to take the outward sea journey a mile off the coast, heading to the area where he and Daniel had spent their last fateful fishing trip together.

Gareth's thoughts were lost in memories of earlier days when they'd both worked together in accounts for a company, and of the friendship bond they'd built at work and in numerous weekends spent sea fishing not only at Falcombe Sands, but other coastal venues around the country. Days when any commitments beyond work were flexible and not tied down.

As time went by, Gareth had started to develop a relationship with Melanie, but he was still able to fit in a fishing trip now and again with Daniel.

Thinking about the past, and then considering the bright prospect of likely promotion at work, helped to make the long drive feel considerably shortened as Gareth pulled into a parking bay at Falcombe Sands marina, where a quarter of a mile away at the beach he'd first encountered Daniel returning as a spirit.

A colourful line-up of sea cruisers and powerboats paraded the jetties. Gareth's twenty feet motorboat was outsized by many of the grander vessels in sight, but it was perfectly adequate for the offshore trip planned.

He entered the wood cabin office of the boat hire company, situated just inside the marina, and after completing some paperwork was escorted by the hirer to the launch.

"Only you on this one?" the man enquired, raising an inquisitive smile on his rugged outdoor face.

"Been attending a conference near here over the last couple of days," Gareth embroidered. "Used to do a lot of sea fishing with a friend years back from here. Just want to unwind for a while in a familiar place after the conference before going home."

Gareth felt the need to make his trip sound plausibly natural, since most would usually share a motorboat with a friend or family. Telling him he planned to meet a ghost was not a feasible option.

The craft, named Belle Maid, featured a white canopy and red hull with open seating at the stern. The hirer gave a demonstration of the controls, though Gareth felt confident of handling the craft with his previous experience of sea fishing.

He set off heading for the approximate area, a mile offshore, where they'd shared their last fishing trip together. The marina and resort shrank behind as the boat cut through the waves, leaving a foaming trail spreading outwards in its wake. It wasn't long before Gareth reached the general area on the water where he and Daniel had cast their fishing lines together for the last time. He presumed the spirit would make an appearance, since the meeting had been requested.

As he waited, Gareth's mind re-enacted the drama that had unfolded ten years ago to the day on the fishing trip with Daniel.

They'd stopped casting and were sitting together on a bench seat at the stern of the boat eating their packed lunches.

"Bet you I'll get the biggest catch today," Gareth boasted, after neither had so far caught anything.

"Well you might," Daniel replied, "but I'm near to getting a very big catch at work."

"In case you hadn't noticed, there aren't any sea fishing opportunities at work," joked Gareth, "unless you mean Dilys Foster, the woman you've been dating. Are wedding bells about to ring?"

"Haven't reached that stage yet, we're just seeing how we get along together at the minute. And I'd prefer you not to compare her with catching a fish." Daniel gazed wistfully out to sea.

"You're a lucky man being engaged to Melanie," he added, watching a seagull circling in hope of stealing a morsel in the event they had a catch.

Both men eat their sandwiches saying nothing for a while, as the boat swayed gently on the waves.

"No, I mean a big catch of someone at work who's been cooking the books," Daniel broke the silence. "I was asked by Ron Peterson, you know, our department manager, to go through some checks on the sales accounts, and let me know if they all added up as they should."

"And did they?" Gareth's interest was aroused.

Daniel turned his head to gaze at his companion.

"No, it looks as though someone is syphoning off money, quite large sums over time, into an account that doesn't belong to the company," he replied pointedly.

"Who is?" Gareth was finding it hard to suppress a hint of panic in the question.

"Now that's for me to know, and you to guess," said Daniel, smiling enigmatically.

"I suppose you'll have to tell Ron Peterson what you've discovered," probed Gareth, annoyed that his companion, his closest of friends wouldn't reveal the identity of the person.

Daniel ignored the query and continued eating his packed lunch, biting into an apple.

"Right, let's get back to fishing," he declared after a few minutes, dropping the apple core into the plastic lunchbox and closing the lid.

Gareth lingered a little longer, continuing to finish his food. His friend may have discovered someone else falsifying accounts and syphoning money into a personal bank account, but Gareth couldn't take the risk of doing nothing. He'd been diverting money from the organisation for nearly a year and not been discovered.

"Are you going to just keep sitting there?" Daniel glanced briefly behind, then cast his fishing line into the sea.

110

"No, I'll join you in a minute," replied Gareth. He was growing anxious. Was it likely Daniel had discovered the accounting discrepancies? Was he going to report him to the department manager Ron Peterson? That would mean the end of his career, probably prosecution, a prison sentence, a criminal record.

He was soon getting married to Melanie. He'd been covering his tracks, transferring money to build up a fund to cover wedding costs, and a sum to put towards a mortgage so they could buy a house. His salary combined with Melanie's earnings were sufficient to live day to day, but not big enough yet to lay out large amounts.

If Daniel revealed his unlawful activity to the department everything would be ruined, probably including his forthcoming marriage. His closest friend wouldn't do that, would he?

And come to think of it, he knew Daniel was fond of Melanie, though had never made any attempts to try and steal her from him. But if he was convicted of a criminal offence? Who knows? It might be the perfect opportunity for Daniel to move in.

Gareth concluded he couldn't take that risk either. Close friendship was one thing, your entire life being wrecked was another.

"I've got a catch!" yelled Daniel, "a big one." His excitement filled the soft breeze, as he began reeling in a fish.

Gareth decided it was also time for him to spring into action. He rose swiftly from the seat and took a few paces across to reach down and hoist Daniel's legs off the deck, tipping his body over the side of the boat. Daniel released the fishing rod as he began to topple, desperately trying to reach back and grab the handrail, but his body's momentum had carried him too far to grip it.

He began floundering in the water, his arms thrashing the surface attempting to stay afloat. His terrified cries for help, in between his head disappearing and re-appearing in the surf, went unheeded. Gareth knew his friend couldn't swim, and cold bloodedly watched the horrific drowning unfold.

The problem of exposure was slipping away, as Daniel made a few more desperate struggles to survive, then finally disappeared beneath the embracing waves.

If he hadn't removed his life jacket because he found wearing it too restrictive for fishing, the instantly formulated plan to dispose of him overboard could not have taken place, thought Gareth.

Naturally he'd have to report the incident when he returned to the marina. To make sure the scenario sounded plausible to the authorities, he unhooked the onboard life jacket attached to the vessel, and tossed it into the sea.

His friend, he would explain, had reached too far over the side in his attempt to haul in his catch, lost balance in the struggle, and toppled over. Of course, he'd tried to save him, throwing the lifejacket, but Daniel hadn't been able to reach it before sinking out of view. It only required Gareth to lie about himself not being able to swim, or else he would have dived in to save him. That would satisfactorily complete the fictitious story.

But it wasn't so easy. The investigating officer didn't accept Gareth's explanation as that straightforward. Something made him suspect there was more to it.

"Where were you on the boat when your friend fell overboard?"

"I've told you a dozen times or more, I was fishing from the other side. I heard Daniel cry 'I've got a catch', and as I turned to see, he seemed to be leaning too far across his side, then lost balance and slipped over."

"Had you been arguing before this happened?"

"No, we were having a great time?"

"Been drinking alcohol?"

"No, we stuck to fruit juice while fishing. We'd planned to go drinking when we got back."

The questions rolled on relentlessly, hour after hour, as the officer and a colleague attempted their own fishing routine for a catch in his story. Gareth wearied, at one point almost near to confession just to escape the onslaught. It was hell, but he held out, eventually being released from further investigation.

The officer thought there was a chance of new clues when Daniel's body later washed up on the shore. However, over the few missing days, the corpse had become bloated and decomposed too far for DNA or bruising evidence to be gleaned, and there were no skull or bone fractures to indicate foul play.

Gareth had got away with it, and the years had lessened the event's impact. Until Daniel's re-appearance.

After reflecting on the past, Gareth began to wonder if Daniel would be making an appearance. Had he made him hire the boat and set out to their former fishing area just for a joke? A fool's errand?

"Hello, old friend," the voice came from thin air, a few seconds before Daniel manifested his spirit body on the bench seat opposite, causing Gareth to flinch. He wore the same yellow short sleeved shirt, blue jeans and dark red trainers that he'd worn on that fateful day ten years earlier.

"Well this boat isn't a patch on the fishing vessel we used last time we were on this stretch of water together, but I suppose it'll do for our purpose," Daniel belittled the hire craft.

"The purpose of you leaving me alone," Gareth reminded.

"Well yes, but we do have a little score to settle, don't we?" Daniel grinned.

"I thought me hiring this boat and meeting you here was the deal for you to stop interfering in my life," Gareth repeated the agreement.

"They were good days back then, weren't they?" Daniel gazed around taking in the waves stretching to the horizon, distant cliffs and the hazy bluish grey shoreline of Falcombe Sands. Then he directed his gaze back at Gareth.

"Made some great catches on our fishing trips, didn't we? Oh, those carefree days."

Gareth stared back at him quizzically. The spirit was sounding friendly, but the laid back tone was leading to something unsettling, of that he was certain.

"Do you know what it feels like to drown? The sheer horrifying terror?" Daniel asked, his manner beginning to harden. The question stunned Gareth, growing fearful of what he was leading towards.

"Of course you don't, you can swim," the spirit smirked. "If I'd hoisted you over the side of that fishing boat, you'd have easily remained afloat and climbed back on the deck." The ghost continued to look at his murderer sitting opposite, seeing him grow pale, fear mounting in his eyes.

"How did you feel watching me drown? Didn't you register any emotion, any regret at seeing me struggling, crying for help, desperately trying to cling on to life before sinking to my death beneath the waves?" Daniel piled on the pressure.

Gareth remained speechless. How could he justify such a wicked, evil act? The incident recalled in such a matter of fact way, increased the impact of the cruelty.

The spirit said nothing now, just observing the guilt in Gareth's eyes beginning to show deep regret for committing the unforgiveable act.

The boat rolled slightly on the waves, riding a patch of turbulence. A couple of gulls swooped low over the vessel in hope of seeing an unattended scrap of food. Detecting none, they curved upwards heading back towards more fruitful pickings on the distant shoreline.

"I was terrified you were going to report me to our boss for skimming money from the company into my private bank account," Gareth broke his silence. "It would have wrecked my future. I'd planned to stop doing it very soon."

Daniel slowly shook his head, expressing disappointment in his former friend's confession.

"Do you honestly think I would have exposed you? Had you no faith in our friendship over many years?" Daniel sounded hurt.

"If you hadn't suddenly decided to kill me, I was soon going to tell you that I'd discovered it was you draining the money, and to stop doing it," the spirit revealed. "That if you stopped, I wouldn't report you. What you were doing was criminal, but no-one else would know if I told Ron Peterson, our manager, there were no discrepancies that I could find in the accounting," he paused.

"And that is because I hid your trail, managing to spread the loss into other budgets, where the amounts would be miniscule, and not enough to raise suspicion." Daniel shook his head again, in disappointment of his old friend's lack of trust in him. "I committed a criminal act to save you!"

The news sent a shock wave through Gareth. If only he hadn't acted so hastily, Daniel would still be alive, and the whole harrowing episode would never have happened.

Gareth lowered his head, cupping it in both hands.

"I'm so sorry, I don't know what to do to put it right," his sorrow poured out pitifully.

"I do," Daniel announced without hesitation. Gareth looked up, hope rising that there was a chance of redemption.

"Take your clothes off," he ordered.

"What?" Gareth looked stunned.

"Well if you don't want me to continue haunting you, then do as I ask," Daniel offered the option.

"Why do you want me to take my clothes off?"

"You'll find out."

Gareth stood up and reluctantly removed his jacket, placing it on the bench. Then his shoes, shirt, trousers and socks, now standing only in his underpants, his remaining dignity only enclosed by the garment.

"I meant everything," Daniel commanded, all trace of friendliness gone.

Slowly Gareth lowered and stepped out of the covering, standing naked on the deck.

"Humiliated me enough have you?" he snarled at the spirit. The remark was ignored.

"Now climb over the side of the boat and get into the sea," Daniel issued his next demand.

Gareth was in two minds. Should he obey, or stop this ludicrous procedure? Get dressed and steer the motorboat back to the marina?

The hauntings. They needed to stop. He'd continue following Daniel's orders for a little longer, but no more. He clambered over the side of the boat and shivered as he lowered himself into the chilly sea.

"It holds no fear for you, does it?" Daniel called, looking down at Gareth bobbing in the swell of the waves.

"Well now I'm a ghost, the water holds no fear for me either. I can go anywhere I like," as Daniel uttered the words he disappeared.

Gareth wondered if undressing and getting into the sea was all that had been required of him. Perhaps he could now climb back into the boat and return home, freed from the hauntings.

Within seconds he felt his ankles being gripped. Something was starting to pull him down. He struggled, flailing his arms in the water, frantically trying to resist the downward haul. He shook his legs, attempting to free his ankles from the increasingly strong grip, but with the sea's density also slowing their motion, it had little effect as a way escape.

His head began to sink under the surface. Soon it was totally immersed. He now held his breath while still struggling to free his ankles. Bubbles rose to the surface, the exertion forcing air from his lungs.

An eternity of time seemed to pass as his increasingly desperate efforts to resurface proved impossible. His chest felt on the point of exploding as he exhaled the last remnants of oxygen supporting life. Unconsciousness enveloped.

Daniel released his hold and now returned to the boat. He sat watching his former friend's lifeless body rise to the surface, face upwards, rolling on the waves. He stared at the corpse for a few minutes, satisfied that justice had almost been done.

Then silvery speckles began rising from Gareth's eyes, forming into an arc and gliding into Daniel's staring eyes.

The flesh on Gareth's naked body began to dissolve, blood seeping into the sea in cloudy swirls. His insides began disintegrating, liver, heart, muscles, sinews, his skeleton following as the silver speckles continued to flow from the eyes of his head, now the only bobbing remnant.

On the deck, Daniel was transferring piece by piece into Gareth's naked form. The speckled arc finally ceased flow-ing, as the head totally decomposed. No trace of the corpse remained, and the swirls of blood diluted in the brine. The transformation was complete.

The new Gareth stood up and dressed in the former owner's clothes, stacked on the bench beside him. The sensation of being alive again was invigorating. He took deep breaths of the refreshing air, felt the warmth of the sun on his body, the sensation of the waves gently rocking the boat.

Now re-incarnated, he realised how the senses of being alive are so incredible. Something perhaps he hadn't fully appreciated in his former existence.

Being a ghost had its advantages of moving rapidly anywhere without any impediments, no barriers, no fear. But it excluded the wonderful gift of touch, enjoying a good meal and drink, the joy of sweet air, lovemaking and so much more as a human being. Of course there were downsides, but that was the deal of living. He meant to make the most of rebirth, and certainly shave off the beard his former friend had grown.

And now the amazing sensations of living movement and power were also reinforced, as he steered the motorboat back to the shore.

He'd noted where Gareth had parked the car at the marina before joining him on the boat, and after returning the craft to the hirer, made his way to the vehicle, taking out the keys contained in the jacket he'd inherited. The car journey to his new home also formed an exhilarating reborn experience.

Justice was now complete he concluded, pulling up on the driveway of the house.

As he climbed out of the vehicle, the front door opened and two children came racing towards him.

"Daddy!" cried Sophie and Amelia, hugging his waist. He ruffled their hair affectionately.

"Did the conference go well?" Melanie approached, reaching out to hug him as the children let go.

"Very well," the new Gareth replied, embracing her and kissing the lips of the woman he loved.

I hope you enjoyed *The Restless Grave*. If you'd like to read more of my books they're listed on following pages and available through Amazon. But first a taste of my paranormal mystery:

THE GHOSTS OF HARCOURT GRANGE

CHAPTER 1

EDDIE settled himself on a park bench. Life wasn't treating him well. His own fault he knew, but it was hard coming to terms with the fact. The blame for his downfall laid entirely on him.

He wondered about his next move, unaware that fate was already mapping a perilous future for him.

A middle-aged man, with side parted greying hair, and wearing a smart dark suit, approached and sat on the park bench a couple of spaces from him.

Both men stared ahead, their eyes following ducks gliding on the park pond, quacking and occasionally dipping their heads for a nibble at food beneath the surface. Strolling on the path in front of the bench, office workers took lunchtime fresh air breaks, mothers accompanied their chattering children.

Eddie's gaze changed to the spread of trees on an expansive lawn at the far side of the pond, thoughts still immersed in his woes. He'd had everything. His wonderful partner, Steph, the business they ran together, and a comfortable flat. Now he'd blown it all.

They'd met at a friend's party. She worked in a baker's shop, and as well as the standard fare of bread and rolls, Steph's wizardry at making delicious cakes became a successful addition to the range.

He worked at a restaurant, starting as a waiter, but progressing to preparing meals by learning skills from an acclaimed chef.

Eddie and Steph decided to leave these jobs, borrow money from the bank and open a restaurant in their Bedfordshire home town of Tollbridge, combining their skills to make meals, exquisite desserts and cakes.

"Lovely day, isn't it," the grey haired man broke into Eddie's memories. He turned and nodded. The bright August sunshine and gentle breeze combined to create a pleasantly comfortable temperature. The stranger smiled, the lines of middle age creasing his face, his eyes searching for communication. Eddie resumed staring across the pond, immersed in his thoughts again.

The couple's new business went well in the beginning. Novelty interest from the townsfolk. Praised by many. But after a few months, customer numbers began to decline. Eddie and Steph couldn't compete with the big chain restaurants on price and special offers.

"Taking a lunch break? the stranger interrupted Eddie's memory again. It annoyed him, but he returned another nod, and summoned a brief smile. Eddie could hardly afford a packet of crisps, let alone lunch. Now he reflected on his current financial status.

The takings for the restaurant began to decline. Eddie had taken charge of the accounts, and assured Steph all was well, even though the deficit began to mount. Secretly he took to online gambling in an attempt to reverse their fortune. It was a hopeless strategy as losses now began to increase on two fronts.

Then Steph opened a letter in the post Eddie hadn't been able to retrieve before her. It was a notification from the bank, that since the loan repayment on the restaurant had not been paid for six months, action was being taken to issue a repossession order.

"Why the hell didn't you let me know?" she screamed at him in their flat above the restaurant. "I trusted you!"

"I was trying to protect you from worrying about it" Eddie pleaded his excuse.

"I saw you doing online gambling sometimes, but I thought you were trying small punts for fun," Steph's anger continued to grow. "You were gambling to try and get repayment money, weren't you?"

Eddie couldn't deny it, and his attempts to calm her were forcefully rejected.

"You bloody fool, driving us towards bankruptcy. I can never trust you again," she shouted. "That's it. We're over!"

Salvation lay in the fact Steph's grandmother had gifted money in her will, which would be enough for Steph to pay off the repayment debt, and put the restaurant up for sale. But she had no intention of helping Eddie any further, even when he told her that his own bank account had been cancelled some weeks before, and without funding from the business account, he'd be virtually penniless.

"I don't bloody care. You made your bed, now go and lay in it," she'd told him, "you're not dragging me down any more. I'm going to stay at my parents for a while, until I can get the mess sorted. I'll be back here later to collect my things, and I hope not to see you here." Collecting her coat and handbag, she'd left.

Eddie continued to gaze at the pond. His depression stunned him into a stupor. How could he have been so recklessly stupid?

"You look rather troubled," the well spoken stranger interrupted his melancholy again. Eddie's inclination was to tell the man to mind his own business. He had enough to worry about, without some nosy parker intruding into his life. But with his emotions being occupied elsewhere at present, he couldn't be bothered to tell the man where to go.

In fact, the reverse happened. Eddie suddenly felt the need to pour out his heart to someone. A confessional therapy. Someone unknown who would likely have no judgemental attitude towards him.

"If you bloody well want to know, I'll tell you why," Eddie declared.

"Please do," the man replied calmly.

When he'd finished the tale of woe, the stranger gazed sympathetically at Eddie.

"We all take a wrong turn sometimes," his confessor observed, hoping to lessen the sense of guilt for him. "Just needs time to repair."

Eddie found himself beginning to warm to this new-comer in his life. Someone who didn't consider him worth-less. Both men looked at the pond again as a flotilla of ducklings glided behind their mother across the water.

"I may be able to help you," the stranger spoke, breaking the brief silence. Eddie was unsure how to react. Help was certainly what he needed, but why would someone completely unknown to him want to assist. The man's expensive looking suit didn't mark him as a roaming charity worker searching for down and outs.

"Why would you want to help?" Eddie posed.

"I've had difficulties in my life," the stranger replied, "and knowing what it feels like, I empathise with you."

"You sound like an educated man," said Eddie, "like you live well off."

"I am and I do," the man admitted, "but that doesn't shield you from difficulties." His eyes appeared to reflect on memories of obstacles in his own life.

They gazed at the pond again. The duck brigade had taken a sweep across the water and now swung round to re-trace their journey. A boy on a bike pulled up on the path in front of them, and leaned over to check the chain. Satisfied it was okay, he rode off.

"If you don't mind me saying, you look as though you've been dragged through a hedge then rolled in the dirt," the stranger said, studying Eddie's clothing.

"You're right," Eddie agreed, taking no offence. After separating from Steph, he had little money on him.

The small amount of cash he'd had in the flat was all that remained. It had been enough to afford two nights in a local bed and breakfast down the road from his former restaurant. But last night he bedded down behind a hedgerow in the park, not far from where he now sat. His only possessions were some clothes and toiletries in the travel bag resting beside the bench.

Eddie had been orphaned at eight years of age after his drug addict parents could no longer cope, and relatives didn't want to get involved. Growing up in an orphanage had put the wider family even further out of reach, so in that direction he had nowhere to turn for help or refuge.

He didn't want to burden a few of his closer friends, who were now living in other parts of the country, and he felt that his pride had been damaged enough without resorting to begging from them.

"I'm fairly wealthy," the stranger interrupted Eddie's drift into memory again. "You can stay at my country house for a while if it helps," he offered.

Any lifeline was welcome, but Eddie felt cautious of a generous offer from someone he didn't know.

"Who are you?" he probed.

"I'm a surgeon, and work at the specialist hospital here in Tollbridge. My name's Ernest Albright," he revealed.

Eddie was surprised to learn of the man's high status, particularly the fact he should be interested in such lowly company.

"I need a gardener and general maintenance man for the grounds of my country estate, and I'll pay a reasonable wage for the work," the consultant continued. "You'll also have your own room and free meals."

The work wasn't anything Eddie had considered pursuing in his life, but the prospect of not living rough was appealing. Trying to find work had been the next on his agenda, and now a job was falling into his lap.

His only worry lay in wondering if there was some ulterior motive for the lifeline offer. But even if there was, the surgeon would hardly be likely to tell him if asked. And right now, he was glad of being offered the refuge.

"That's really good of you," he said, accepting the offer. "I'm Eddie Cartwright."

"My pleasure," the consultant smiled, stretching out his hand to shake Eddie's. "I have a flat in town here," he continued, "where I'm largely based during the week near the hospital. My main home is near Coulton Regis in Sussex. The residence is called Harcourt Grange. Been in my family for generations."

Eddie was impressed. Ernest Albright came across as a man of great knowledge and wealth.

"Thing is," Eddie paused, feeling embarrassed, "I don't have enough money right now to get to your place in Sussex. I can hardly afford a bus ride across town."

The surgeon reached for his inside jacket pocket and produced a black leather wallet. Opening it, he counted out a generous amount of notes, more than enough for the train journey involved.

"That's for your travel from the station here, as well as a good meal, new shirt, shoes and trousers. I don't want you turning up looking like a tramp." He handed the money over.

Eddie's first thought on receiving it was that he could just walk away and spend it how he liked. Gamble it even. But that had only brought about his downfall, and the offer he'd received seemed to be a much better prospect for the time being. The surgeon gazed at him with invasive eyes, as if reading his thoughts.

"Thanks," said Eddie, giving a smile to indicate he could be trusted. "I'll catch the train today."

"There's one that leaves at 3.10 this afternoon," said the surgeon. "You'll have to make a change at Albany Station, and that'll take you directly to Coulton Regis," he said, standing up.

"I'll telephone ahead and tell my wife Edith to expect you. Our driver will collect you from the station," he added, and left.

Eddie finds himself in a very strange house, where he begins to fear for his life. Read what happens next in

THE GHOSTS OF HARCOURT GRANGE

Available on Amazon

DEAD SPIRITS FARM

Evil spirits await the new owners of a haunted old farmhouse.

THE LOST VILLAGE HAUNTING

Ghosts rise from an old fishing village that long ago fell into the sea.

EMILY'S EVIL GHOST

Ghosts reveal murderous horror in a haunted country house.

CURSED SOULS GUEST HOUSE

Where the only guests are ghosts, waiting for new arrivals to join them.

DARK SECRETS COTTAGE

Shocking family secrets unearthed in a haunted cottage.

THE SOUL SCREAMS MURDER

A family faces terror in a haunted house.

THE DARKNESS IN PHANTOMS

Phantoms unleash terror in a strange new world.

THE BEATRICE CURSE

Burned at the stake, a witch returns to inflict revenge.

THE BEATRICE CURSE 2

Sequel to the Beatrice Curse

A GHOST TO WATCH OVER ME

A ghostly encounter exposes horrific revelations.

A FRACTURE IN DAYBREAK

A family saga of crime, love and dramatic reckoning.

VENGEANCE ALWAYS DELIVERS

When a stranger calls – revenge strikes in a gift of riches.

THE ANARCHY SCROLL

A perilous race to save the world in a dangerous lost land of myths and legends.

THE TWIST OF DEVILS

Four short stories of evil devilry.

MORTAL TRESPASSES

A mysterious phone call leads to a secret sect rais-

ing the dead.

All available on Amazon

For more information or any questions please email:

geoffsleight@gmail.com

My Amazon Author page:

viewAuthor.at/GeoffreySleight

Tweet: http://twitter.com/resteasily

Your views and comments are welcome and appreciated.

Printed in Great Britain
by Amazon

26609211R00076